Assumptions and Other Stories

By James Mulhern

Copyright © 2016, James Mulhern

ISBN-13: 978-1523318599

Published by James Mulhern

Acknowledgment

I would like to acknowledge the following for their support of my writing through the years: Maureen Mulhern, Kathy Scherpa, Amelia Costigan, Ann Bauer, and most importantly, James Cennamo.

Dedication

This book is dedicated to my
brother Mark, the best pal I ever had.

Contents

ASSUMPTIONS 1

THROUGH A CONVENT GATE....................................15

THE MANNEQUIN...21

SMOKE RINGS...40

MYRA BOCCA...47

A PRAYER FOR HOME...70

DRENCHED TO THE BONE 106

Assumptions

"You are altogether beautiful, my love;
there is no flaw in you."
(Song of Solomon 4:7)

Peggy Fleming, according to my grandfather was the "homeliest damn woman" he'd ever seen. Her face was swollen and pasty, with broken capillaries that sloped down the sides of her nostrils, flooding the arid plain of her skin, like some dreary river and its tributaries eking over a delta of nasolabial folds to terminate in the red seas of two droopy cheeks. Spindly, awkward limbs stuck out of a round body, like you might see in a kindergartner's rendering of a person. She was, unfortunately, toothless, and hairless as well, suffering from a mysterious childhood disease that had left her with chronic alopecia. Peggy used to tell us kids that she lost all her hair because she refused to eat green beans when she was a child. I always thought it a cruel irony that she had the same name as the graceful and beautiful skater who had won the Olympic Gold Medal in 1968.

I remember hearing my grandparents and Auntie Ag, my grandmother's older and "much smarter" sister (the one who graduated high school), likening Peggy's features to those of a bulldog, as they puffed away on Lucky Strikes and Parliaments, stopping every now and then to slap down a poker chip or a playing card, and take another sip of whiskey. While they played cards, I circled the kitchen table and listened, picking up snippets about Peggy's tragic life.

Her story goes something like this--She was married once to a very handsome man named Jim, who was quite successful in business, something to do with cutting pants--"slacks" my grandmother called them--for a good company. Everyone was surprised that Peg could get such a catch, but like many ugly people, she had a heart of gold, and oh could she sing! The two of them, they met in a nightclub in Boston's Back Bay, one of those divey joints, nothin' too swanky, where Peg performed for a small crowd on Friday nights. She sang those good old songs from back in the day, songs like "Fools Rush In," not the crappy remakes, but the *best* version with Frank Sinatra, and other songs like "You Stepped Out of a Dream" by Sarah Vaughan (that broad could pull your heart strings). Jim often stopped by the nightclub after work, and you know, eventually they hit it off, and one thing led to another, and of course they got married. But by Christ! How in God's name could Jim stand to look at that puss day in and day out?

And wasn't it a tragedy, how one evening, after a game at Fenway Park, Jim drove the green Buick that he loved so much into a fruit stand on the side of the road, killing the old Italian guy selling the stuff, and himself, of course. Afterward, Peg was never the same. She wouldn't go out, still hardly does, and that was years ago. It's a shame how she's tried to drown her sorrows by cozying up to that bottle. It's a good thing she has a neighbor like Helen to check on her, and take her out once in a while.

And Helen, my grandmother, would beam at this point, say something like, "Well, the poor thing!" Then Auntie Ag would nod her head in disgust at the whole terrible situation, and Grampie, he would become stone silent, ashamed to have said so much already.

In the knotty pine basement of Peggy's home was a beautiful Steinway piano. My most vivid memory of Peg's singing was when, after my grandmother and she had a few highballs, they led me down the cellar stairs so that she could sing for me in front of the piano. My grandmother had bragged, as most grandparents do, that I was a most talented pianist, and Peg wanted to share her own talent with me, encouraging me that I could "make it" like she had someday.

They were both very drunk; I was relieved that neither of them had fallen down the stairs and broken their necks. My grandmother goaded Peg to sing "When Your Old Wedding Ring Was New," Peg's favorite.

With one thin arm braced against the polished black surface of the Steinway, she sang with no accompaniment, and even now, years later, I hear the swelling sadness in her voice, remembering too, the indignity and shame that I experienced when my grandmother slyly smirked at me and rolled her eyes. Peg was horrible, of course--years of smoking, drinking, and heartache had ravaged her vocal chords-- but her pain was so real. I knew that she was dreaming--longing for her husband Jim--and I think it was then that the first throb of death's glower entered my consciousness.

During my childhood years, I would learn more about Peggy's life. While my grandmother prepared dinner, Peg minded me in the parlor, regaling me with her stories. She grew up in Jamaica Plain, an Irish catholic enclave in Boston. Her cousin, Mary O'Malley had sponsored her trip to the States back in the thirties. "Terties," Peg would say in her brogue. Mary had preceded her from County Mayo fifteen years earlier, marrying a young "whippersnapper" named Joseph Conner whom she'd met at one of the socials, weekly gatherings in the basement of Saint Thomas More Church. Joseph worked nights at South Station loading mail onto trains for the post office, while Mary worked as a maid during the day, cleaning the houses of the "filthy rich on the hill"-- Mission Hill she meant. Mary and Peg's relationship had been like that of sisters.

When the Conners began having children, Peg became their trusted nanny. "I couldn't have children of my own," she told me. "Those years were some of the best in my life. Funny you don't know such things until it's past. I should have stolen Francis," she said. "He was my favorite. You remind me a bit of him sometimes. He became a priest, a missionary to a small town in Italy, where he died in a church. What luck! Don't you think?"

Peg was a talker. I was fascinated by her stories, especially her tales of the wee people who harassed her on the way to school. "By the brook was where they most appeared. They'd be hiding in the bushes, beautiful Gorse Bushes with bright yellow flowers. The little buggers were quick, and if you weren't fast, they'd catch you and pinch you to death." She shuddered dramatically at the thought of it, then whispered, "I think that's who pushed Margaret Mary Fawny off the cliff. She was this nasty girl who made fun of me. What a jinnit she was! Slapping my face when Sister Ignatius wasn't looking, and calling me a toad. Can you imagine that, Jimmy?" I shook my head, wondering, too, what a jinnit must be. "What must she have thought as she fell through that cloudy air?" Peg murmured. "I hope she had time to say a Hail Mary or two before she drowned in Achill Sound." She laughed.

"I'm just codding ya, Jimmy, just an old story is all. A fib, my love," she said, reacting to my frightened expression. "And I was ugly, ya know, but it was horrible of her to taunt me just the same."

"You're not ugly," I said.

Peg laughed. "Oh, that you were forty years older! You're a charmer, you are."

When the ice in her glass had melted, or the whiskey was getting low, she'd motion for me to take it. I learned to pour her whiskey sours at the kitchen table. My grandmother, who was usually chopping vegetables or tending to food on the stove, looked over at me. "Not too much, sweetheart," she'd say. "Tell Peg our supper is almost ready."

When I was ten, my father sent my dog to the pound because he barked too much. Of course I cried, and phoned my grandmother, who had just come from lunch with Peg. The two of them arrived within the hour, scolded my mother and cursed my father, who was still at work. A few hours later, we had retrieved Scruffy from the Animal Rescue League of Boston. During the ride back, my grandmother and Peg convinced me that the best thing was to find a new home for the dog.

"To hell, with your father," Peg said, passing me a sugar cube that she kept in her pocketbook in case her insulin dropped suddenly. "We saved Scruffy's life, sweetheart. And what matters most, Jimmy, is knowing that he's happy. Sometimes that's the way it has to be, my love."

At my grandmother's house, Peg took charge, calling the local radio stations and asking would they broadcast that "the sweetest dog Scruffy" needed a home. She and my grandmother drank several whiskey sours during their home-for-the-dog campaign, and I'm certain that the disc jockeys did not take Peg seriously, let alone understand her. She was slurring her words, calling Scruffy "Ruffy," or forgetting his name altogether, sometimes dropping the phone to pick up her drink with both hands. Once she referred to him as a cat. She cursed the "sons of bitches" that hung up on her, and every once in a while scratched the back of Scruffy's head, which rested on my knee.

"You'll see. Everything will be alright," she kept telling me.

We had Chinese food delivered, and at the end of our meal, Peg opened a fortune cookie and read, "Do you believe? Endurance and persistence will be rewarded." For Peggy, this was a mystical sign that we should "get off our arses" and knock on doors all over the neighborhood. "Where there's a way, there's a will. What we need is faith is all, and our coats," she said, smiling at me.

"Surely, they won't refuse the request of a cute little boy," she told my grandmother.

My grandmother said she was too damn tired to go traipsing around the neighborhood, and passed out on the couch. Peggy said, "To hell with you, too, then!" and laughed.

The three of us--Peg, Scruffy, and myself--began canvassing the neighborhood. It was December and cold; the sky was crystal clear. I could see my breath, and just above us, one very bright star seemed to be chasing a crescent of moon. What a sight we must have been! Peg zigzagging beside me, me nudging Peg--trying to keep her from falling off the curb, Scruffy following behind, wagging his tail and sniffing spots along the way.

We walked several blocks that night, ringing bells and knocking on doors on both sides of the street, stopping a few times to plan what we should say. Peg said that what we needed was a hook. She suggested that she could take off her wig and tell the people "just a little white lie" about her dying of cancer. I said that I thought that was probably a mortal sin, and my grandmother wouldn't like it. She agreed with me, so we decided to state the simple facts, "No blarney. Just the bit about your father sending poor Scruffy to the pound."

Some people didn't answer their doors. It must have been after 10 pm, and I imagined tired strangers peeking out at us, annoyed to be disturbed at this time of the night. Of the people who listened to our tale of woe, most were gracious and polite. Some of the neighbors clearly recognized Peg though, and there were looks of exasperation and disgust on their faces.

"Take the boy and his dog home," one young mother said. "It's too late to be out, especially with you in the state you're in. You should be ashamed of yourself. It's freezing out here and the boy's going to catch a cold."

"But the dog needs a home!" Peg pleaded.

"The *boy* needs a home even more. Now take him home before I call the police and have you arrested for public drunkenness." She gave me a pitiful look before shutting the door in our faces.

"Show me the way to go home. I'm tired and I wanna go to bed," Peg began singing, "I had a little drink about an hour ago and it went right to my head. . . . "

"Have faith," she told me, "We'll find a home for him. You know I'd keep him if I could, Jimmy, but I'm all allergies. Makes my face puff up and screws up my breathing." In addition to alopecia and diabetes, Peg suffered from episodes of acute asthma.

My grandmother was snoring on the couch when we returned. Scruffy jumped onto the wing-tipped chair, and curled himself into a ball. Peg and I serenaded my grandmother with "You're Nobody Till Somebody Loves You" until she awoke with a start and asked for her "damn" drink.

The rest of the night is a blur. Perhaps I fell asleep on the rug watching t.v.? Maybe my grandfather carried me to bed when he returned from his night job? What I remember most about the events of that evening is that Peg kept her promise. Later that week, she found a home for Scruffy--with a "rich doctor" at the clinic where she used to get all her medications. A couple times over the following months, she took me to see him. I was content--he had a large fenced-in yard, and there were other dogs as well. I was happy to know that he was happy. Peg had been my savior.

A few years later, my grandmother brought my sister, Peg, and me to be cured in the waters of Nantasket Beach. Snapping open her compact that morning, she peered into the mirror while she smothered her lips with red, all the while explaining the importance of August 15th to Beth and me. We were seated in her kitchen, sunlight flickering on the orange-and-gold checkered pattern of the wallpaper behind her.

"On August 15th," my grandmother elaborated, "we celebrate the Feast of the Blessed Mother's Assumption, when Jesus's mother, was taken to her heavenly home."

"Who took her?" Beth asked.

"God, dear."

"In an airplane?"

"No, sweetheart. Finish up your eggs."

"Then how'd she get there?"

My grandmother rose and began washing dishes at the sink.

Beth and I looked past her head through the window to examine the sky.

"It's a mystery, Bethie. Just one of those things," she said at last.

"Oh." Beth said, picking up her fork. "A *mystery*."

Throughout that hot August day, I would catch Beth staring at the sky, looking for traces of Mary. I was on the hunt too, spotting flying Mary's everywhere, flares of white light in my peripheral vision that would disappear as quickly as I turned my head.

The dogma of the Assumption, I later learned, was firmly established in 1950 when Pope Pius XII made his decree: "We pronounce, declare, and define it to be a divinely revealed dogma; that the Immaculate Mother of God, the ever Virgin Mary, having completed the course of her earthly life, was assumed body and soul into heavenly glory." I've always wondered why it took so long to decide on the fate of poor Mary, who like a participant in a tableau vivant, remained motionless, one foot on the earth and one foot in the air, for centuries.

On this Feast day, according to Irish Catholic tradition, there is a cure in seawater. In Ocean City, New Jersey, for example, the priest would lead a procession to the shore after his mass, where he, accompanied by a lifeguard, got in a small boat and rowed out a short distance to lay a wreath on the waves and make a benediction. Some have suggested that the tradition is an assimilation of the Celtic festival of Lughnasadh, begun by the god Lugh--the deity associated with late summer storms and lightening--as a funeral feast commemorating his foster mother, Tailtiu, who dies of exhaustion after clearing the plains of Ireland during the harvest. Back in Ireland, I've been told, many people continue to celebrate this August holiday with bonfire and dancing. The Irish have a proclivity for morbid thoughts and martyrdom; and I am not surprised that this holiday is an amalgamation of exhaustion, death, martyring motherhood, food, and a cure.

While at Boston University, I remember flipping through the art book of a housemate when a copy of Titian's *Assunta* caught my attention. A startled Mary, arms spread above her upturned face, is being lifted on a cloud toward heaven, where God waits expectantly, his gray beard flowing in the turbulent air. Mary is surrounded by angels, excited as flower children in the church before a wedding. It is difficult to tell whether the crowd of apostles below is reaching to pull her down or to push her upwards. The depiction is unnerving;

you can almost hear the commotion, as if someone has just cried out, "Wake up!" "Last call for alcohol," or "The baby's coming." The cloud, which you'd expect to be a soft fleecy white, is a cradle of thunderhead gray; in the background the sun blazes a fervid yellow. The painting's most vivid colors are orange and red, shades of fire, flesh and blood.

My grandmother revered the Blessed Mother; there were statuettes and pictures throughout her home on Kendall Road in Braintree, Massachusetts. She used to tell me that her favorite month was May, the Blessed Mother's month, and that she had the good fortune of being "born in May and married in May." I can still picture my grandmother as she waved goodbye to me from the corridor of the elderly housing apartments where she ended up. Next to her, on the windowsill, was a blue marble carving of Mary.

The idea of a "cure in the water" paled in comparison to the roller coaster ride that my sister and I, if well behaved, might enjoy at Paragon Amusement Park across from the beach. Since we weren't sick and didn't need a cure, "Mary's blessing" seemed like a gyp.

After our breakfast, the three of us--Beth and I wearing bathing suits under our t-shirts, and my grandmother arrayed in a white and gold sundress, a wide-brimmed hat with a spray of lilies, and black Farrah sunglasses--crossed the street to get Peggy, who had been "very ill" lately. I had overhead my grandparents whispering about Peg's "delirium tremens," how she was imagining things, and telling crazy stories about monkeys calling her up on the phone. One night a police officer brought her to my grandmother's house after he found Peg wandering the streets of a nearby square, bruised and beaten-looking. Peg had said that she was looking for her husband Jim, trying to bring him home. I remembered our cold walk in December and wondered if Jim had been on her mind even then.

In the bag that I carried were six baby-food jars to collect salt water for our family, some clusters of red grapes, as well as apples, raisins, and a few banana loaves that my grandmother had stolen from Solomon's Bakery, where she worked part time. My grandmother believed it was a mortal sin to waste the day-old baked goods, even though the management had insisted that they be tossed in the rubbish.

Just outside Peg's door, my grandmother stopped us, licked her fingers to arrange the bangs on Beth's forehead, hair that my grandmother had cut earlier in the day. When my grandmother wasn't around, Beth complained to my mother, "She cuts crooked, and then she tries to fix it, but it always makes it worse. I look dumb! Make her stop!"

"Now don't you stare at poor old Peg, and no giggling," my grandmother warned Beth before knocking on Peg's door. "She's not herself, and we need to help her get better."

"And Jimmy, remember to call her 'Lovely Peggy,' " she whispered to me quickly. 'Lovely Peggy' was the sobriquet my grandmother had invented one Sunday after a sermon the priest had given on the power of names and the mystery of the Word. If we thought lovely things about Peggy, she explained, Peggy's life would be happier, and she would feel better. "You kiddos don't know how much this visit means to a lonely old lady."

Peg opened the door. I mechanically announced, "Good morning, Lovely Peggy."

Peggy responded, as she always would, "Isn't he adorable," while Beth skirted past her into the kitchen, desperate to get away, and my grandmother, appalled at Peg's appearance, said, "What's the matter with you? Did you forget we were going to the beach?" She looked down at Peg's feet, tsk-tsking at what Peg was wearing. "You look foolish in those things."

Peggy had a confused look on her face, like she was half-asleep. There was pure grief in her expression, as if she felt cheated from a surprise. Her housedress, which had a pattern of tiny roses, shrouded a pair of small black boots; there were red stains at the end of her sleeves from where she had spilled some juice. She had forgotten her wig and the sunlight highlighted a laurel of peach-fuzz hair; a few long silver strands, moist from sweat, garlanded the area by her temples and behind her large ears. The blinds were pulled down on the window beside the kitchen table behind her, and the sweet smell of cedar cabinets and wine surrounded us in a cloud.

My grandmother crossed the threshold, flicked on the lamp, and guided Peg to the table. I hadn't seen Peg in several months. Her usual cheeriness had vanished, and she was distracted and distant. It unnerved me to see how much she had changed. I joined my sister who was seated on the verdant green divan in the living room, strategically positioned in front of the dish of hard candies that we had grown accustomed to raiding on our visits.

We were quiet, enjoying the deliciousness of peppermint candy, swinging our legs together and humming just a little, eavesdropping on the conversation from the kitchen table, which was not far from where we sat.

"Let's have one for the road, Helen."

"You've had quite enough already, Peg. Aren't your feet hot in those God-awful boots?"

"Not really."

"But your feet must stink. You've got to take those damn things off! The salt water will be good for your gout and all that puffiness around your ankles. And the water will help the calluses on our soles!"

Peg laughed. "I figured the boots were perfect for the beach."

"For Christ's sake, Peg! The point is to get wet. How else are you going to get the cure?"

"Cure for what?"

"Well, anything. Your aching bones, your mood, your bowels, whatever it is that's bothering you, Peg. *God* will know what you need. Miracles do happen, ya know." I pictured my grandmother making the sign of the cross, Peg watching dreamily. I don't know that Peg was very religious. I'm not even sure if she was a practicing Catholic, but that wouldn't have stopped my grandmother in her missionary zeal. She had a strong faith, and would often remind me that my first prayer should always be for the Holy Father's Intention that the Catholic Church reign forever. If you were not Catholic, as far as she was concerned, you were going to hell.

My sister and I listened intently to their exchange. I knew from past experience that their bickering had become a ritual, and I was hoping for a good fight, anything to make Peg seem more awake, more like her old self.

"I believe miracles sometimes do happen, Helen," Peg said at last. "It will only take me a moment to get ready. I have to use the little girls room and put on my fancy wig and makeup so I can look divine for my Jim over there," she said. Her eyes seemed teary, but she smiled and winked directly at me as she looked past my grandmother towards where Beth and I sat in the living room. The chair creaked. She groaned and tried to lift herself up; we rushed to the doorway so we could have a better view.

"I need to straighten out," Peg said, arching her back.

"You're fine, Peg. You're fine." My grandmother helped her through the narrow doorway and down the hall. Peg hesitated every now and then, pressing her trembling palm against the wall, as if to discern whether it, or she, was still really here.

There was no arguing that day that I can remember. We drove to Nantasket Beach, Beth and I singing along to Carole King's "You've Got a Friend" on the radio, getting bored when my grandmother switched channels to listen to the talk shows that she liked so much. There was discussion of McGovern, Nixon, Peking, Vietnam, and all that money wasted in sending a man to the moon. The sun flashed on the blacktop of the Southeast Expressway. I moved my head to the open window, smiling as the wind washed over my face. Beth held up one of the glass jars to admire its sparkle.

It was breezy at the shore. My grandmother managed to coax Peg out of the boots, pouring salt water playfully over Peg's toes before leading her into the ocean; but that was after a gust had lifted Peg's wig into the air, and the four of us, laughing uproariously, chased it along the sand. At last, Beth caught the wig, then raised it in the air like the head of John the Baptist, giggling and tiptoeing a slow dance across the sand. I took it from her and smoothed the sad hair before burying it in the paper bag with a stone I had found near the water.

Soon we found a comfortable place on the beach. My grandmother rubbed tanning oil into Peg's bald scalp, forehead, and the nape of her neck; she shone like a miniature Sun. Peg let Beth and I drape a necklace of dried seaweed upon her; we pretended it was a string of jewels. Then the two of us scribbled words into the sand with our fingers and played Yahtzee until we lost one of the die. The salty north winds felt good against our skin, and Peg kept wrapping our shoulders with her purple towel so we wouldn't get burned.

Later, as Beth and I waded through the shallow waters at the ocean's edge, we stopped occasionally to work and wedge our feet into the cool sand, then sloshed our legs through the foam a bit, deliberately making heavy giant steps and dancing to keep pace with the sun. We splashed ourselves as we jumped to avoid dark clumps of seaweed or a jellyfish, and we scanned the hard bottom for a lonely starfish or stone, or the clam with a secreted pearl. For a while, we explored large rocks that edged the beach, unearthing small crabs in the sand between, and startling a mourning dove that sped from its cleft into the bright sky. It made a whistling sound as it rose; then it began to descend over the water where my grandmother and Peg were walking towards the ocean. The waves beyond glimmered like sparks from an unquenchable fire. On a jetty in the distance, a father and his son cast fishing lines into the sea.

Suddenly, we heard my grandmother shout, "Watch yourself!" but it was too late; both she and Peg were surprised by a spirited breaker that razed them in its wake. Of course we ran to help, but delighted, too, in the spectacle--my grandmother and Peggy, seated on their asses, just a few feet from where the waves trickled to their end. In an instant they were kneeling forward, laughing so hard that they cried. As we began to help lift them, my grandmother and Peg, in between guffaws, groaned that the soles of their feet were cramping from shells and stones beneath their feet. My grandmother said that her "permanent is all ruined" while she fussed with her hair. Peggy answered, "At least I don't have to worry about that," and they laughed even harder. Then Lovely Peggy reached for me. I was mesmerized by her wet silvery scalp, and resisted the urge to touch the crown of her head before I gave her my hand and she rose from the sea. "Jimmy, you're my angel," she said, and kissed me on the forehead.

We filled six jars with water that day, and starving, we made a feast of the bread and fresh fruit by a small tide pool in the shade of a bony cliff. In the late afternoon, Beth and I had our roller coaster ride. With hands shielding their eyes from the sun, my grandmother and Peggy waved to us, transfigured figurines on the earth below, their clothing white as snow. The coaster lifted our chariot further into the crystal sky, while on the horizon, the deity Lugh tried to wake us all up, turning heat lightening on and off behind a lacey curtain of gray. And still his mother slept beneath the dusty harvest loam.

It has been a long time since that ride, but when I recall that afternoon, I feel the heady anticipation of the rising, and the delightful fright of the quick fall. Only a few days later, early on a Sunday morning, my mother would come to my room and wake me. She sat on the side of my bed where I had propped myself against a pillow. When she told me that Lovely Peggy had died in her sleep, I felt the pang of grief, but a sweet happiness, too, as I remembered our December journey, Peg's persistence and her songs.

I imagined Peggy "over there," eyes no longer teary, her countenance reflecting the brightness of a blazing fire. Finally she would be at home with her Jim. Completely awake--laughing, altogether beautiful, and divine--she rises once again to sing her favorite song. And the Sun's great light shines upon and caresses her warm skin, like the flesh of a Father's hands as He cradles His child's head before lifting His crossed arms to kiss her soft cheek. A Father, joyful and tearful at the same time, hallowed by a loveliness that would forever be a part of Him.

"Feast of the Assumption, 1924"
by Fr. John Duffy about his beloved mother Bridie

You shamed that naked goddess of the seas,
0 Bridie, barefoot in Our Lady's tide
The day you begged a miracle to ease
The swollen feet that life had crucified.

Clothed to the knees in black, you stood and prayed.
Your little son, I watched, appalled. I knew
What you were praying for and was afraid
Of God and miracles and even you.

Ah, back you came, cheated of your surprise,
A crone bent over, cramping on shells and stones,
Our Lady's answer grieving in your eyes
And Golgotha still groaning in your bones.

Nothing, poor dear, poor crone ... But what you thought
Blessed back to God what lust had cursed away,
And with the aching in your bones you wrought
A sacramental out of Quincy bay.

I'd carve you in great marble if I could,
My Bridie of Our Lady of the Sea,
To show the sorrow of it, how you stood
Praying in vain for what was not to be.

Long dead, my dear... but when at last we meet--
O changed forever! The Eternal's bride,
Robed all in white down to the little feet

Shining like His who once was crucified!

Through a Convent Gate

"What a shame," Nonna said when I arrived at her place after working at the family restaurant. "Mary Muldoon just called. Drunk as a skunk, asking if I knew where her husband Jim was and quite annoyed at the Happy Garden Chinese Restaurant. Said they were sending her pork fried rice and egg rolls at least three times a week. Claims she never ordered a thing."

"Where's her husband?"

"He's dead, Molly. Has been for years. She found him in the living room around dinner time. Massive heart attack."

"Oh, that's terrible."

"She must be having blackouts and forgetting things. Or she's imagining that they are delivering the food. Mary has squash rot," Nonna said. "Poor thing. Her mind's all messed up."

"What's 'squash rot' ?"

"It means your brain is rotted from too much alcohol. When she drinks, Mary gets delusional and hallucinates."

"She eats at our restaurant once a week. Never says much unless it's to complain. She's nasty to me. And she told my father that I'm a 'clumsy oaf' and should be washing dishes instead of serving food."

Nonna said, "You've got to have compassion for her, Molly. She's been through a lot. Can't help herself. Addiction to alcohol is a terrible thing."

"I don't think it's an excuse to me mean, Nonna."

I excused myself, saying I had homework, and went to her bedroom where I would hang out until my parents closed the restaurant.

Nonna thought it would be charitable of us to visit Mrs. Muldoon around Christmas time.

We walked precariously up the steps of Mrs. Muldoon's front porch on a late afternoon in December. "Mrs. Muldoon will slip and fall on this snow," Nonna said. About two inches had fallen that morning. "Grab that shovel against the house and clear a path from her door down to the street."

It didn't take me long; the snow was light and airy. I shoveled while Nonna gave commands. As we were stomping our feet and about to ring the doorbell, the door opened. "Aren't you going to clean the curb, too?" Mrs. Muldoon said to me. "I like to walk on the street you know. The slobs next door never clear the sidewalk."

"Of course she will," Nonna said, and then to me, "Molly, just finish up that little bit while I go inside with Mrs. Muldoon. Then join us." Mrs. Muldoon held the door as Nonna entered.

"You'll do a good job, won't ya?" Mrs. Muldoon said with a fake smile. "Not make a mess of it like you do sometimes at the restaurant."

As the door shut, I gave Mrs. Muldoon the finger. Even though she didn't see my gesture, it gave me pleasure. I shoveled the curb, making sure to leave just a bit of snow on the curb, hoping she might slip.

I found the two of them standing in the archway that led to the living room. Nonna was oohing and aahing over a silver aluminum Christmas tree with a color wheel.

"I love those red and green balls, and the see-through ones, too." Nonna commented. "Isn't it pretty, Molly?"

"It's gorgeous." I wasn't that impressed.

"Well the damn thing ought to be. Paid a pretty penny for it. At Sears, ya know. The girl in the store, a pudgy midget, said it was a specialty item."

"Oh, a specialty." Nonna winked at me. "Well it's beautiful, Mary. Now why don't we go into the kitchen and enjoy some coffee while we eat the cookies I brought you."

"I don't know why they call it a specialty item. They've been around for years," I said.

"Well it's special to me," Mrs. Muldoon snapped. "Where are the cookies, Agnella? I could use something sweet to get rid of the bad taste in my mouth," she said, looking at me. We walked into the kitchen.

"I wrapped a few up and put them in here." Nonna patted her black leather handbag.

"Well I would think you could give me more than a few. What are you? Cheap?"

Nonna laughed. "Mary, you got the diabetes to worry about."

"Was she really a midget?" I interjected.

Mrs. Muldoon looked irritated.

"Molly's asking about the salesgirl in the department store." Nonna smiled at me.

"I know what's she's asking, Agnella. Yes, Molly. Or a dwarf. I don't know what ya call them nowadays. But nice enough, she was. And quite knowledgeable. She told me the tree was made in some town in Wisconsin. Would be an heirloom in the future. I said to her, 'I don't care about any heirlooms, dear, and I don't care about the future. I haven't got a soul to leave it to.' And don't ya know, the midget said to me, 'I'm sorry.' I said, 'About what, darling?' And then she said, 'That you haven't got any children.' I laughed and told her not to worry. Children could be a pain in the arse. Isn't that right, Molly?"

Mrs. Muldoon almost slipped on the red-brick linoleum floor, but Nonna was able to grab her arm and steady her into a chair. The kitchen smelled like pine. Nonna explained later that the smell was from all the gin that Mrs. Muldoon drank.

Nonna brewed coffee in the percolator, after rummaging through the disorganized mess of cupboards. Mrs. Muldoon was silent, her eyes dreamy, looking out the window above the sink.

"Mary, where's the sugar?"

"Look on top of the refrigerator."

"Crazy place to put it," Nonna said, taking the yellow sugar bowl and placing it on the table.

"It's starting to snow again," I said, following Mrs. Muldoon's eyes. "Guess you'll have to find someone to shovel for you later on, too."

"It is, and isn't it pretty? Do they still make snowflake cutouts in school, Molly? I used to love Christmas time when I was a tot."

"Mrs. Muldoon, I'm a senior in high school. They make snowflakes in elementary school."

"What a shame," Mrs. Muldoon said. "People at every age should make snowflakes. That's a joy of Christmas. Don't you agree, Agnella?"

Nonna was pouring the coffee and arranging the anisette cookies on a plate. "Yes, Mary. Snowflakes should be appreciated at every age." She opened the refrigerator and sniffed the small carton of cream. Her nose crinkled. "Mary, the cream's gone bad." She poured it down the sink and ran hot water. "We'll just have to have our coffee black."

"Let's have a gin and tonic instead," Mrs. Muldoon said. "Molly, too. She's a *senior in high school* now," she said, over-enunciating and smirking. "Too old for snowflakes." She laughed.

"We're having coffee. No alcohol. Wouldn't go with the cookies," Nonna answered.

"Snowflakes form in the Earth's atmosphere when cold water droplets freeze onto dust particles. The ice crystals create myriad shapes. No two are alike," I said. "I think that's more wondrous and beautiful than anything we could create with scissors and white paper."

Mrs. Muldoon laughed. "Aren't you a whippersnapper. And all those big words: *myriad* and *wondrous.* " She humphed.

Nonna set the coffee and plate of cookies in the table center. "Molly's very smart. She got a perfect score on her SATs. Her IQ is 148, almost genius level."

"Whatever that means," Mrs. Muldoon said. "What else do they teach you? Do they teach you to count your blessings? Do they teach you your catechisms? Do they teach you the Ten Commandments, the Our Father, and Hail Mary? Now those are valuable lessons." She picked up rosary beads and laminated novenas that were on the table. "Faith is most important, Molly." She shook the beads.

"Yes, of course they teach us those things, Mrs. Muldoon. The sisters have to explain all of that to us. I'm not sure I believe any of it."

"What do you mean?" Mrs. Muldoon said. "So sacrilegious. And at this time of year." She tsk-tsked. "Now there's a big word for you." She laughed and sipped her coffee, then glared at me. "You are not smarter than God, Molly." She placed her cup down firmly. A bit of the coffee spilled over the rim.

"I think that Molly is saying she's a free thinker," Nonna piped in.

"A free thinker? What a bunch of malarkey. I don't even know what it means."

"It means she makes up her own mind about what she believes.

She's an independent young woman."

Mrs. Muldoon guffawed.

"Let's change the subject," Nonna said. "No need to be arguing."

"I suppose you're right, Agnella," Mrs. Muldoon said, raising herself from the chair. "I've got to use the little girl's room anyway." Nonna helped her stand.

"I'm okay, Agnella. Stop being such a mother hen."

Nonna laughed. When Mrs. Muldoon left the kitchen, Nonna whispered to me, "Go into the living room and get me a few of those see-through balls from the tree."

I did just that, bringing her two translucent balls and one red one. "I like the red one," I whispered. Nonna wrapped them in napkins and stuffed them in her bag, which she clasped shut just as we heard the toilet flush down the hall.

Mrs. Muldoon returned. "I was just thinking about Vivian Vance. It's sad that she died. Oh, how she used to make me laugh."

"Who's Vivian Vance?" I said.

"Ethel Mertz. You know. From *I Love Lucy*. Now that was a funny show. And Lucille Ball. What a riot!" Nonna smiled.

"God bless the people who make us laugh," Mrs. Muldoon said.

"I wonder what a dead body looks like. I'd love to see one," I said.

"What an odd thing to desire." Mrs. Muldoon pursed her lips.

"It's sad that Vivian Vance died, but I don't see why her death is any more tragic than the death of anyone else," I answered. "Do you know there's approximately 153,400 deaths per day, or a little more than 100 per minute? Just think of how many people died while we've been sitting here. We are all specks of dust floating in an enormous universe."

"Your granddaughter is getting too big for her britches. Imagine? 'Specks of dust.' I don't even know what she's talking about half the time. Wanting to see a dead body, too? Where does she come up with these things? Jesus, Mary, and Joseph!" She took a sip of coffee and looked out the window. The black bark of a tree cut through a gray square of sky.

"Don't mind her, Mary. Molly's just a thinker."

"I could tell her a few things to think about." Her things sounded like "tings," and her think sounded like "tink." I was going to correct her but Nonna said, "We should get going. The snow is falling. And Molly's got homework to do. Don't you, Molly?"

"Yes, Nonna. And I want to add some more ornaments to our Christmas tree so it can be just as beautiful as Mrs. Muldoon's."

"Yes, yes," Nonna said, rising from her seat. "It's a beautiful tree."

Mrs. Muldoon guided us to the door, commenting some more about my poor attitude, and then as we walked home, Nonna said, "Such a shame. An old woman drinking herself to death." She stopped suddenly and turned to me. "You've got to learn to hold your tongue. Learn not to be so fresh."

When we hung the ornaments on our tree, Nonna said, "She won't notice them missing. And it's a shame not to have them appreciated. Don't you agree, Molly?"

"Yes, Nonna."

Later, as I lay on Nonna's bed doing homework, I picked up the phone and called the Chinese restaurant.

"This is Mrs. Muldoon again," I said. "Send me over an order of pork fried rice, egg rolls, and add some beef broccoli this time. And you'll hurry it up, won't ya? I'm so hungry I could eat a nun's arse through a convent gate."

The Mannequin

After I showed my paperwork to the girl at the desk and signed in, David, an upperclassman at Boston University who was helping freshmen move in, brought me to an elevator in the rear of the hall. In the short time it took to get to the fourth floor, he managed to tell me a bit about the alleged haunting by Eugene O'Neill. Shelton Hall was once an apartment building, and O'Neill and his wife Carlotta, whose psychiatrist had an office on Bay State Road, lived in suite 401 starting in 1951. Eugene died of Parkinson's disease in 1953.

David said, "His last words were 'Born in a hotel room and goddammit, died in a hotel room,' " as we reached the door of my suite, a pair of bedrooms (each shared by two females) with a common area. I was having trouble with the key; it wouldn't turn.

"Let me help you with that, Molly." He placed his warm soft palm on my wrist. His hands were big with long delicate fingers, like those of a guitarist. I noticed how clean his nails were and I could smell his body odor—a mix of sweat and freshly baked bread. I felt my nipples harden. Maybe he would be my second? I thought. And I hoped he would be better than my first, a boy from my high school American History class, who I later found out was gay.

The door swung open quickly. We walked through a drab common area with the same azure blue carpet from the hallway. There was an old red-and-white plaid couch, an electric stovetop, and a small t.v. My room, which was labeled A, was on the left. This time the key worked well. My roommate had already moved in; her things were on the left side of the room, the section with the best view of the Charles River. My side was close to the bathroom, which

I wasn't crazy about, and was darker with poor overhead lighting.

David pushed the bin to my bed, which was covered by a navy blue spread and two lumpy pillows. "It's not the best," he said, "but the view from the ninth floor is spectacular and the dining hall serves pretty good food."

"Actually, I think the building is charming. I've always wanted to live in downtown Boston."

"Guess your roommate's name begins with an A." He nodded towards a very loopy pink wooden A that hung on the wall above her dresser. On the top shelf of the bookcase beside the dresser was a gold metal crucifix and a picture of what I assumed was her family. All of them were blond—father, mother, brother, and her. There was even a yellow Labrador retriever.

David followed my eyes. "She looks pretty vanilla. Almost seems like one of those fake photographs that comes with the frame."

"Let's look. Maybe it is." I laughed and he stood close as I pulled the cardboard backing from the frame and took out what was an authentic photograph. On the back was written, "Mom, Dad, Joey, me, and Saint Paul."

"Who the fuck is Saint Paul?" David laughed. He hovered over my shoulder and I smelled him again. I wanted to kiss him.

"Must be the dog, unless it's her brother. But he doesn't look like a saint. He looks like a pain in the ass."

"It's my dog." The voice came from behind us. David jumped.

We both turned. A pear-shaped, very tall Ashley stared at us with an irked expression. Her blond over-permed hair reminded me of a poodle and she had gained at least thirty pounds since the picture was taken.

"Sorry," David said, putting his hands in pockets. "The picture just looked so perfect. We thought it was one of those fake ones that comes with the frame." He smiled and laughed--flawless white teeth.

"You had no business touching my stuff." Ashley stormed forward and grabbed the picture from the bookshelf. She pulled up the bottom of her pink t-shirt to rub off our fingerprints, then she slid the photograph inside of the cardboard backing, pushing down the clips, and held it tight to her small chest.

"Lighten up," I said. "It's not like we were going through your panty drawer." I extended my hand to shake hers. "I'm Molly Bonamici. This is David. He's one of the helpers for students moving in today." She turned and put the picture on her bed in between two stuffed teddy bears, as if that would protect it from future affronts. She had a fat ass that made the green and pink lines of her plaid shorts even uglier.

"Aren't you going to shake my hand?"

"Not right now," she said. "I'm still pissed off, but my full name is Ashley Adams."

"I guess I'll get going." David raised his eyebrows at me.

I thanked him. He winked at me before he walked out the door and mouthed, "Good luck." I loved his smile.

Ashley busied herself unloading a bag of construction paper, glue, scissors, and markers onto the desk by her window. I walked to my side of the room and checked out the bathroom. It was old-fashioned with black-and-white subway tile on the floor and white painted walls. There was a claw-footed bathtub with a black shower curtain, a decent size medicine cabinet, and 6 black shelves on the wall. I splashed water on my face, and wiped my hands on my jean shorts.

When I came out of the bathroom, I found Ashley lying on her bed, reading a book entitled, *The Elements of Language Curriculum.* I opened my suitcase and began putting my clothes away in the oak laminate dresser, hanging some things in the closet on my side of the room. "Are you an education major?"

"Yes," she answered without looking up. "I'm in the College of General Studies."

She couldn't be too bright. Students who are not outright accepted to Boston University are enrolled in the General Studies College, a sort of probationary acceptance, with matriculation later on. "What grade level are you interested in teaching?"

"Elementary." She flipped a page and pretended to read.

"We need good elementary teachers. One of my favorites was Ms. Hopkins. I can still remember her beehive hairdo. I think I had a crush on her."

Ashley looked up at me, frowning. She fingered a gold cross around her neck.

"Oh, I don't mean 'crush' in that way. I'm not a lesbian if that's what you're thinking."

"I wasn't thinking that." She looked me over, eyes moving up and down. "Where are you from?"

"Revere. I am from a *very* Italian neighborhood, not too far from here."

"Where's that exactly?"

"Just outside of Boston. About five miles to the north."

"Can I ask you a personal question?" Ashley shut her book.

"Sure."

"Do you know any people in the Mafia? . . . One of my parents' favorite movies is *The Godfather.*"

"The stereotype of the Italian Mafia is mostly hype from movies and books. But to answer your question—yes. One of my Nonna's friends, Mr. Scarfone, has ties to the Mafia. He's involved in small-time things like gambling, money laundering, and drugs. Nothing major. He doesn't smash horse heads onto bedposts." I laughed.

"That's scary." She straightened her back and rubbed the top of her hand.

"Not really. If you met Mr. Scarfone, you would like him. He seems like a nice old uncle. He tells stupid jokes, but he's always smiling and kind. . . Where are you from?"

"Lenox, Massachusetts. We are mostly white so I don't think we have a lot of Italians."

"I see. . . .That's where the Boston Pops plays during the summer. I've always wanted to go to Tanglewood."

"Both my parents are violinists," she said.

"That's cool. I like classical music."

"I hate it." She put her book down and sat up on the side of her bed, watching me put my books on the shelves. "Did you read all of them?"

"Yes."

"I hate reading long books. I prefer children's books and young adult fiction."

I knew we were not going to be friends. I couldn't help thinking she was an idiot.

"Oh, and I like the Bible, too." She tilted her head upward, tossing her poodle-do with one hand. I noticed a pimple on her chin.

"I don't like the Bible much. Mostly it's a bunch of bullshit. The New Testament isn't all that bad. I like the Gospel of John, especially its Prologue: 'In the beginning was the Word, and the Word was with God, and the Word was God.' The idea of words being portrayed as divine appeals to me. I'm an English major, and of course I love books."

"But it's not words that the Gospel is talking about," she said. "

'The Word' means Jesus."

"I don't think so."

"Of course it does." Her face flushed. "John was talking about *Jesus*."

"That's an interpretation."

"Are you a Catholic?"

"I'm an atheist. I think religion is the cause of most of the world's troubles."

"How can you say that? Jesus died for our sins." Her voice was shaking.

"Ashley, I doubt you are an expert on the Bible. But let's change the subject. Have you met our suitemates?"

She slid back on the bed and propped herself up with pillows, moving the teddy bears and picture aside. "No. They haven't arrived."

"I wonder where they are?" I said, thinking, please let them be more interesting than this *stunod,* as Nonna would say.

"Maybe they're coming from far away. BU attracts students from all over the world." She sounded like she was reading a brochure.

"Yeah, maybe they are coming from Mali or Guinea."

"I never heard of those cities. Is Guinea where guinea pigs are from? I think they are so cute."

"They are not cities. They're countries. Both in Africa."

"Oh."

"This is soooo adorable," someone said, entering the common area. The voice was that of an older woman--raspy, and slightly nasal.

"That must be one of them." Ashley bounced off the bed, patted her t-shirt, and fluffed her hair. "How do I look?"

I laughed. "You look fine."

"Well, don't you want to meet them?"

"I think we should give them a few minutes to get settled. Is it okay if I use the bottom three shelves in the bathroom?" I wanted to put my toiletries away.

"I guess so." She was hesitant.

"Or would you prefer the bottom shelves? I just figured because you were taller, the top shelves might be easier for you to reach, Ashley." I wanted to call her Lurch, as in the *Addams Family*.

"That's fine. You can have the bottom shelves." She looked at herself in the mirror on the back of our door, smiled, and walked into the common area. I moved just aside the door to hear the conversation.

"Mom, it's hideous. But that's fine. A college room is not supposed to be the Ritz."

"Emily, turn around. One of your suitemates is here," Emily's mother said.

"I'm Ashley. Ashley Adams."

"Emily Finnegan. And this is my mother."

"Just call me Lorna."

"Nice to meet you both," Ashley said.

"You too, darling," Lorna answered.

There was an awkward silence. I wished there was a peephole in the wall so I could spy.

"Well, I guess we should continue moving my things in," Emily said.

"Oh, I can help if you like."

"No sweetheart. Go set up your own room. I'm sure you have a lot to do as well," Lorna said. It was obvious that Emily and her mother wanted to get rid of Ashley.

"Really, it's no bother."

Emily said, "Actually I prefer to move the things in myself. Plus there's a guy downstairs who's offered to help, and my sister is waiting by our car. So we have to hurry. We'll talk later."

So Emily didn't seem to care much for Ashley either. I had a feeling that she and I were going to be friends. At least we had one thing in common—an antipathy for Ashley. Ashley came back into our room and shut the door tightly. I quickly opened a dresser drawer and pretended to arrange my pants. I could hear voices in the bedroom next to ours, but the words were indistinct. I got the sense that Emily was unhappy with the dorm, college, or something else going on in her life, and her mother was trying too hard to make everything seem wonderful. I've always been intrigued by the inflections of emotion in people's voices. Most emotions felt like foreign languages to me, but over the years, I had become very good at translating them and reading people. Sometimes, I would reenact conversations I'd overhead, watching my facial expressions in the mirror.

"They were a bit rude." She sank into her bed and folded her arms. Her t-shirt lifted slightly, revealing her white belly.

"Why do you say that?"

"I offered to help them move in and they brushed me off."

"Maybe they just wanted to spend some time together. You know, the whole mother-daughter thing. Child leaving the nest."

Her face was steely. "I think she's a bitch."

"Who? The mother or the daughter?"

"Well I guess both of them."

"Don't you think you are being a bit harsh?"

"I was just trying to be a good Christian and offer help."

"Atheists can be good, too, ya know." This girl was really starting to annoy me. I started brainstorming ways to avoid spending a whole school year cooped up with her. "Christians don't hold a copyright on goodness."

"I didn't say they did."

"No, but you implied it." I pulled a pair of black panties out of my drawer and placed them on top of my dresser. Then I walked over to the mirror and began to disrobe, tossing my black t-shirt and cut-off jeans onto the bed. I fluffed my long brown hair, which was a bit sweaty, threading my fingers through the sticky sections. Ashley pretended to read her textbook, but I knew she was watching my antics. I decided to give the prude a show. I unclasped my black bra, shimmied out of my black panties, and threw them onto the bed as well. I turned and faced Ashley—full frontal nudity. "Do you think I have nice breasts?"

Her face was blotchy. She looked up from her book, feigning a nonchalant glance. "I guess so."

Then I put my hands under my breasts, cupping them. "I like them. I think they are the perfect size. 36 C. I like my vagina, too, especially the dark thick hair around it." I scratched my pubic area.

Ashley threw her book on the floor. "Do you have to talk so much about your body? I really don't care that you like your titties."

"Wow." I walked over to my dresser and eased my legs into the fresh pair of panties. "You're so uptight. I would think you'd appreciate the beauty of the human body. After all, the human being is one of God's creations. And I think he thought pretty highly of us because he made Adam lord and master over all of the animals. You should review the book of Genesis, Ashley. I have to pee. Excuse me." I went into the bathroom, leaving the door ajar so she could hear the tinkling of my urine.

I continued putting my belongings away; Ashley pretended to

read. After a while she dozed off. I would have fallen asleep, too, if I were reading *The Elements of Language Curriculum.* From my bed I watched her face for a while. Her mouth was wide open and she was snoring lightly. I walked over and stared down at her. She must have been dreaming because her eyelids were fluttering, indicating REM sleep, a fact I had learned in Health class. There was drool pooling in one of the corners of her mouth; her lips were chapped. Her body was so limp and helpless. I imagined smothering her face with one of my pillows, like a murderess in one of those tacky made-for-t.v. movies that I loved so much.

I quietly opened her dresser drawers, periodically turning to see if she was close to waking. I rifled through her panties, silly underwear with images of Winnie-the-Pooh, hearts, and one with Christmas bulbs. She had an entire drawer of preppy sweaters and turtlenecks—a medley of lime green, navy blue, forest green, red, and black—all made of wool or 100 percent cotton fabric. There was a black velvet blazer, which I found unusual considering the other apparel, flowery knee-length skirts, and denim pants from L.L. Bean.

I heard a loud snort, so I turned quickly, bracing my hands on her dresser. Ashley opened her eyes.

"I must have been exhausted. Was I snoring?" She rubbed her cheeks with her palms and blinked a few times.

"Yes. You were very loud." She wasn't.

"Oh, sorry. I hope it isn't too much of a bother, but I'm sure you will get used to it. You can buy some earplugs. Everyone in my family snores." That was a sleepover I would definitely turn down.

"Hey, why are you standing by my dresser?" She sat up quickly. Her textbook fell to the floor. "Damn." She leaned over and picked it up. I saw the crack of her white fleshy ass. One of her teddies toppled over the other side of the bed.

"I was concerned about you," I said. "Your breathing sounded irregular."

She placed the book on her bedside table. "Really? What do you mean irregular?" The area around her eyes twitched, and I forced myself not to smirk, affecting a serious expression.

"It's no big deal. You're alive. At least for now." I laughed.

"Do you think there's something wrong with me?"

"Don't tell me you're a worry wart, Ashley."

She stiffened, her back firm against the headboard. "I'm not a *worry wart*! That's silly. I was just asking what you meant exactly."

"Methinks she doth protest too much."

"Huh?"

"*Hamlet.*"

"I read that. Edgar Allan Poe, right?"

"Yes. I'm impressed by your knowledge of literature."

She smiled. "Well, that's why I decided to become a teacher. I believe I have a vocation. I am determined to help children grow up and become intelligent readers so their lives can become enriched by the myriad works of great literature." She pronounced *myriad* as MY-ree-ad.

"I'm sure you will succeed."

The courses at school were too easy. I was enrolled in a Freshman Composition class, Intro. to Psychology, The History of Western Civilization (in 562 pages), which I zoomed through, and Major Authors I (most of the material I had read). I had always been in the advanced classes in high school, even skipped a grade. My I.Q., my Nonna liked to brag, was 148. I called Nonna a few times to let her know how things were going; she agreed that Ashley was a prig and wished she wasn't my roommate. "You deserve better. But don't worry, *mia bambina,* those types always get their comeuppance."

I did end up befriending Emily. She was a pretty girl with an atypical, but lovely face. Oval-shaped, flawless skin, kewpie-doll lips, a small quivering chin, and large eyes, like tarnished gold coins. I admired the way she exuded purpose and conviction. We hung out together quite a bit, exchanging stories about our lives, enjoying each other's company.

Emily's roommate, Candice Kox (her real name) from California, never showed so Emily enjoyed a large private room for the semester. I was envious. Ashley had become a thorn in my side, making snide comments on a regular basis about my personality and habits. She was a neat freak and complained about petty things like my hair in the sink or my unmade bed. I had even overheard her calling me "Molly, the pig" in a phone conversation with her friend Jean. I wanted my own room like Emily.

I couldn't stand Ashley's self-righteousness, the way she would come back from the university chapel after mass with a smug look on her face, dropping comments like "God is good" and "Every day is a blessing." She wanted to get under my skin, and she did, insulting me several times in the most passive aggressive manner. I kept my anger at bay, though, confiding only in Nonna. I did not want others, especially Emily, to know my nasty, vindictive fantasies. I would find a way to make Ashley pay for the continuing disrespect.

One afternoon three weeks later, the Resident Assistant called Emily and me to inform us that packages were delivered for both of us. When the phone rang, we were watching the evolving love affair of Luke Spencer and Laura Webber in the soap opera *General Hospital,* arguing over whether Luke was cute or not. I thought he was too old and ugly for Laura. But I didn't care for her much either—she was too histrionic and breathy for my taste, a crisis junkie—so I told Emily that Laura deserved the ugly toad. Emily said I was mean.

She was laughing when she picked up the phone. "Hi Arnold. . . . . . . Really? How big?. . ." She looked at me from beyond the open door to her room. "She's with me now. I'll tell her."

"We have some mail downstairs. Two large boxes for me, and a smaller package for you."

"Let's go. I'm sick of looking at his bad perm." I turned the television off and we went downstairs. Arnold loaned us a dolly to bring up Emily's boxes.

When we had set the mail down in our common area, we both excitedly opened the packages. Hers were from her mother, and mine was from Nonna.

Emily let out a scream and jumped back when she opened the first box.

"What is it?"

"Oh God. My mother sent me a mannequin. It scared the shit out of me." She put a hand over her heart. After she caught her breath, she pulled out the plastic torso of a female, followed my limbs, hands, and a head. At the bottom, her mother had thrown in a brown wig. "She is so crazy!" She opened up an envelope from inside and read the note aloud, " 'Baby, couldn't resist buying this mannequin. Found it in a clothing store on Park Avenue.' " Emily paused and looked at me. "That's Park Avenue, Rochester, not Manhattan." She continued reading. " 'I figured you could name her after your no-show roommate and prop her on the bed to keep you company. Hope you are well. Don't spend all the money too soon.' " Emily pulled a check out of the envelope. I was curious how much, but didn't ask. The second box was the waist, legs, and feet. We screwed the mannequin together and baptized her "Candice Kox" after the missing suitemate.

"She looks like you." Emily laughed.

"She looks like how I feel sometimes," I said, laughing. "Like a cold heartless bitch."

"Open your package." Emily stared at Nonna's cursive on the brown paper she had used to wrap the package. Inside was a Tupperware container full of chocolate chip cookies. There was also a note and a check for $500.

"Well read the note," Emily said.

I could smell Nonna's Shalimar perfume on the light blue stationary. "Dear Molly. Here are some cookies for the sweetest cookie in my life. You must swear to eat them all yourself! Don't give any to your dorm friends, especially that roommate with the stick up her ass. I am very worried about how skinny you have become. A curse on you if you don't eat every last one. I want you to be fatter the next time I see you. I'll send you more money for second semester, or call if you need any. Nonna loves *mia bambina*."

"She sounds very sweet. I never knew my grandmother. She died before I was born."

"Nonna's pretty special. She raised me for the most part. My parents were always so busy with the restaurant they own."

We heard the key in the lock.

"Stuff Candy in the boxes. I don't want Ashley to know about her. I'll explain later," I whispered. The thought of having Ashley joining our fun irked me. She had made a comment that implied I was a whore when she overheard me telling Emily about what happened with David. "Sex before marriage is a sin," she said with disgust, "and I would be ashamed to admit it." I had to bite my tongue. I wanted to ream her a new Christian asshole.

Later, Emily congratulated me on my restraint, and suggested that I just avoid discussing anything personal in front of her. I thought Ashley's beliefs were idiotic, but I had more important things to accomplish than educating a moron. You can't change the thinking of a stupid person, so you find alternative ways to deal with them. Nonna was my sounding board.

"You two look suspicious." She was carrying a bag from 7-Eleven. "I bought some snacks if you want them." Then she saw the cookies. "Oh, but it looks like you already have some. Those look really good."

"They're from my Nonna. I'd give you two some but my grandmother made me *swear* I'd eat them all myself. She thinks I'm too skinny."

She looked at my body. "I wish I looked like you. I think you look perfect. I gotta lose weight. I just wish I wasn't such an overeater." She went into the bedroom and closed the door.

"She deserves credit. She's always watching a VHS tape of ladies in leotards doing something called Fitness Dancing. She confessed to me that sweets are her weakness and she just can't resist, especially during her workout sessions. Said the sugar motivates her." I stood up and ran in place. "She does this with two one-pound weights in her hands."

"How long?"

"Three minutes max. Then she collapses on the bed for a while and afterwards eats from her stash of Entenmann's cookies."

"I hope she doesn't eat your cookies. Your grandmother would be upset."

"I doubt it. She's a Christian, remember? When she reads Nonna's note, I'm sure she wouldn't dare."

I helped Emily slide the boxes of Candy into her bedroom and said I would tell her about an idea for an O'Neill haunting game when we met up with Michelle and Mark, other students from our floor, at dinner. Michelle was a tall, heavy-lidded black girl from Brooklyn, always dressed in flashy orange, pink, and yellow; she hoped to become a famous actress. Mark was an obese white guy with frizzy red hair, blue eyes and a cherubic face, who wanted to become a screenwriter. We always met at 6 p.m. at the back of the dining hall.

It was Burger night. The dining hall smelled of bacon, cheese, grilled onions, and French fries. I was continually impressed by the food at BU. Every night they had a different theme—Asian, Vegetarian, Italian, even Lobster Night. I got a very well-done burger with cheddar cheese and French fries; Emily had her burger with no cheese. She smeared a lot of mayonnaise on her bun, which I found repugnant. I was more traditional—a ketchup kind of girl. When I was a kid, I pretended it was blood.

At the table, Michelle and Mark were discussing President Carter's alleged sighting of a UFO in 1969.

"He's a smart man. There has to be some validity to the idea of extraterrestrials. What do you girls think?" Michelle said. She had ketchup on her chin. I handed her a napkin and pointed.

"I believe in intelligent life elsewhere in the universe, but I absolutely don't believe these extraterrestrials are anywhere near earth. In fact, sometimes I think there is very little intelligent life on earth, period. And if there were such beings visiting from somewhere in the universe, I'm sure they wouldn't want to mix with us; we are much too stupid." I bit into my burger. "This cow was probably smarter than at least thirty percent of Americans."

Emily laughed.

"How do you explain all the UFO sightings?" Mark said. "There's gotta be something to them."

"Forget about the extraterrestrials." Emily waved her hand dismissively. "We have ghosts to talk about." She turned and looked at me. "So what is your plan, Molly?"

I told Mark and Michelle about the mannequin. "I was thinking we could begin phase one of an O'Neill haunting game. Test it out on Ashley."

"How? . . . Can you pass me the salt, Emily?" Mark asked.

"I'm going to David's tomorrow for dinner. We're ordering pizza. I have an idea for when I'm gone."

"Oh, he's the hot blond guy," Michelle said. "Hmm. Wonder what you two will be doing after you eat?" She smirked.

"Discussing the meaning of life."

"Yeah, honey. Just don't create any life."

"Molly, I'm dying. Tell us what the plan is," Emily said.

"Okay, you got to know a little about O'Neill's life. I did some research this week. Evidently, he got angry at his daughter Oona for marrying Charlie Chaplin. She was eighteen and Chaplin was 54!"

"Ugh. That is gross," Michelle said. "She obviously married him for his money."

"I was thinking you could put a cane in the mannequin's hand, a Charlie Chaplin hat on her head, and a nametag that says Oona."

"What the fuck type of name is Oona? Are you sure that's right?" Michelle squinted her eyes and retracted her neck.

"Yes. I'm sure. And what does it matter. Ashley certainly doesn't know."

"Molly, where are we gonna get a cane and hat?" Emily said.

"Oh that's no problem." Mark knocked over his coke. Michelle sopped it up. "Sorry. . . ."

"Jesus, control your enthusiasm." She rolled her eyes as she moved the napkins over the puddle.

"My roommate is studying to be an actor. He has access to the prop room for the BU Theatre. I can ask him," Mark continued.

"And when I'm at David's place, you can position the mannequin in front of the door, knock a few times, hide in the corner and project a high-pitched voice saying something like, 'Hi, I'm Oona. Have you seen my father Eugene O'Neill?' "

Mark said, "Oh my god. She's going to be scared to death."

We laughed.

Emily said, "I don't get it. Why don't you want to help us do it, Molly?"

"She hates me enough. I don't want her to think I had anything to do with it. But I *do* want to walk in on the scene. Ashley exercises every night from 8:30 till 9 pm while she watches that stupid aerobics tape. That way you can be sure she's in the suite and not off studying, or over her friend Jean's. Stage it for 8:45. I'll be walking down the hall from the elevator when it happens."

"Okay, I'm in," Michelle said. "I hope Ashley has a sense of humor."

Emily and I looked at each other.

"We'll see," I said.

Sex the second time with David was not as exciting. I get bored easily. After I've tried something once, the novelty quickly wanes. He asked me why I was in such a hurry so I told him about our plan. He thought it was ridiculous, but wished us good luck nevertheless. At 8:42 I got off the elevator. I saw Mark trying to position the mannequin, which tumbled over a few times before he got it exactly right. I was disappointed that Oona was not wearing Chaplin's signature derby hat. In its place was one of those conical jester caps with bells. At least Mark's roommate was able to obtain a cane. Michelle and Emily were laughing, squatting in the hallway by the next dorm suite. I stood for a few minutes in front of the elevator, pretending to look for a key in my purse. Two girls with grocery bags got out and smiled at me, then headed towards their room in the other direction. They did not notice the scene I had been observing.

I looked at my watch, then glanced to where Mark was pounding on the door. I scanned the hall, hoping no one else was around. Mark dashed to where Emily and Michelle sat. Ashley opened the door wearing a pink leotard, pink stockings, and white sneakers with pink laces. She was eating one of my chocolate chip cookies, holding the Tupperware container. I thought, "Bitch. I told you not to touch them. But you did. I knew you would."

Emily projected in a high squeaky voice, "Hi. I'm Oona. Have you seen my father Eugene O'Neill?" Ashley let out a shrill scream, then collapsed onto Oona, moaning for a bit. Michelle threw a set of bells she was jingling against the wall and ran towards Ashley, followed by the others. Oona/Candy's head came off and rolled down the corridor. Emily kicked the wig and cap into the air. Mark picked them up and said, "Oh Jesus! For the love of God, let her be okay! Oh Jesus!" I hurried towards them.

"Ashley, are you alright?" Michelle said, her face sweating. No answer. Emily was ashen. Mark ran around in a circle, looking at the ceiling, repeating "Oh shit! Oh shit!" twisting the cap and wig in his hands. Every so often there was a jingling of bells.

I flipped Ashley over and checked her neck pulse; there was none. I yelled, "Somebody call 911." Then I began administering CPR, after I wiped her mouth clean with my shirt.

Doors opened up and down the hall. "I already have," a hysterical girl with mascara streaming down her face yelled.

I kicked what remained of Oona to make space and she completely fell apart. My adrenaline was rushing and the force of my punt caused one of her hands to fly and hit the mascara girl in the stomach. She screamed, "Her hand has come off!" Sobbing, she ran into her room and slammed the door.

I was counting my compressions, the heel of one had over the center of Ashley's chest, my other hand on top of the first. I tried to keep my elbows straight, remembering Ms. O'Rourke, my Health teacher's words.

"Mark," I shouted after the thirtieth compression. "Stick your finger in her mouth. Make sure her airway is clear and there are no bits of cookie."

He grimaced and held his head back as he slid his middle finger inside.

Michelle said, "It's not like she has fangs, and she won't bite you. She's barely breathing." She pushed his wrist. "Come on now. Move that finger around. Pretend it's a twat. . . .I'm sorry, that was inappropriate. I'm just freaked out."

At times like this, everything happens so fast. Arnold, our RA, was soon there, as well as the Boston University police. Students getting off the elevator were told to get back on and go to another floor. I continued my chest compressions alternating with breaths, trying not to press my lips too firmly against her mouth. Her breath smelled like nail polish remover. It seemed the lights in the hall glowed for a second, and there was a foul smell of gas. Ashley had shit her pants. I knew she was dead.

"Good job, Molly," Emily said, holding her nose.

When the paramedics showed up, they took over but to no avail. They placed her limp body onto a stretcher. I stood back with the others. "How could this happen?" I said, "Ashley is so young!" Arnold hollered at the crowd of students, "Get back in your rooms." People quickly obliged. Doors shut all around.

I turned to look at Emily who was ironically, "tossing cookies" onto the azure blue carpet.

There was a patrolman looking on, even firemen, and in a short while, a Detective Corrigan from the Boston Police. Arnold escorted Emily, Mark, Michelle, and me down to his office on the first floor. Detective Corrigan eyed each one of us during the elevator ride. He was a scary-looking man with a craggy face, a perpetual scowl, and hollow cheeks. His color was gray. I thought he looked half dead himself. No one spoke until we were all seated in Arnold's office.

There were three folding chairs that I let the others sit on. Detective Corrigan sat in the cushy leather chair behind Arnold's desk.

"Do you want me here?" Arnold said to him.

"No. I want to speak with them alone."

Arnold seemed relieved and left quickly. I grabbed a box of tissues from Arnold's desk and handed it to Mark, motioning for him to pass it on. He gave it to Michelle, who wiped the sweat off her face. Emily grabbed a few tissues and daubed tears on her cheek and puke that had smeared on her sneakers.

"I wouldn't worry about your sneakers, young lady. We have more important matters to attend to." The detective's voice was menacing and his black eyes darted over each of our faces.

"You," he said to me.

"Yes, sir."

"You seem pretty calm. Aren't you upset?"

"Of course I'm upset, sir. I just don't show my emotions much."

"What's your name?"

"My name is Molly Bonamici."

"Since you seem the most controlled of your friends, why don't you tell me what happened? And by the way, what you did was pretty heroic. Where did you learn CPR?"

"High school."

"And you remembered exactly how to do it?" His eyes widened, two black holes.

"Detective Corrigan." I stared at his nametag, then into his eyes. "I don't forget things."

He moved forward, putting his elbows on the desk, interleaving the fingers of his hands underneath his chin. "Okay, Molly. Tell me what happened."

I told him about the alleged haunting of our floor by Eugene O'Neill. He asked me if O'Neill was a former student, with no seeming knowledge of the playwright. When I said he wrote *Long's Day Journey Into Night,* he snapped that I should get to the point before this became a long day's journey into night. He had to file the paperwork before the end of his shift.

"Who's this Oona?"

"Oona is Eugene O'Neill's estranged daughter?"

"Is she a student here?"

"No, she's dead."

"So does she haunt your floor, too?" He was twirling a pen in his hand, reclining in the chair.

"No, she's a mannequin."

"Excuse my French, Molly, but what the fuck are you talkin' about?"

Michelle widened her eyes, as if to say, "don't piss him off." Emily was on the verge of laughing.

Detective Corrigan barked at her. "This isn't a joke. A friend of yours is dead."

Mark looked down, tapping his foot and picking a scab on his hand.

At last, Detective Corrigan got the information he needed for his file. But before he left, he lambasted all of us, saying what we did was terrible and we'd have to live with it for the rest of our lives.

Mark burst into tears. The scab on his hand was bleeding a little. Emily and Michelle recoiled, backs stiff against their chairs, speechless.

"Yes, Detective Corrigan. I realize we will all live with this for the rest of our lives. We are truly sorry that a silly joke ended in Ashley's death." The image of Oona the mannequin in an electric chair flashed in my mind.

After he left, Arnold came back into his office. He was more sympathetic.

"I know you've been through a lot. I've spoken with the authorities, who will contact Ashley's family. You have to be aware that that there could be some disciplinary action. The dean was, well, very pissed off. Expect to meet with him soon. You can go." He opened the door for us.

I waited until the others had left, then said, "Arnold. I was the one who came up with the idea. If there is anyone who deserves the blame, it's me. I don't want my friends to be expelled."

He laughed softly. "Molly, I doubt any of you will be expelled. It was a stupid prank that led to a senseless death. And what you did upstairs was remarkable. We are fortunate that you kept your cool and administered CPR while your friends were in meltdown. You tried, and that's what matters. You showed great strength in a crisis. I couldn't have been as calm as you."

"Thank you, Arnold."

He patted my back as I left. On the elevator, I thought about my actions. I was sure that there were others who would have done the same thing. Nonna certainly.

Ashley was a bitch. Obtaining cocaine from Mr. Scarfone, the mobster friend of my grandmother's, was easy. I had read 1.2 grams of coke ingested orally was sufficient to kill a person. And no one would ever know the real cause of Ashley's death. She had confided in me about her heart condition, Long QT syndrome, which is passed on genetically and would have likely caused her to drop dead some day.

Her family, being very religious, was staunchly opposed to autopsies. One of the perks of being a sociopath is that you learn how to easily gather necessary information by manipulating people, using their weaknesses to your advantage. I knew Ashley loved sweets during her workouts and I had placed the cookies on top of my dresser, the direction she faced while doing her "fitness dancing." I also knew that whenever she paused or was interrupted, she ate a cookie. Ironically, Ashley and I had something in common—a genetic inheritance. I guess you could say we both had heart conditions. Of course mine was more useful. Sociopathy wouldn't kill me.

Nonna was always saying that she would do anything for her

"precious granddaughter," so when I asked her put the lethal dose of cocaine in each cookie, she said, "Sure *mia bambina*. What's one more ingredient? Not a problem." Being just like me, she understood my needs.

Once in my room, I would call to thank her, and remark on the effective wording in her note. Ashley's Christian values had evaporated in the face of temptation. Like Eve, she had eaten the forbidden fruit. Nonna would be happy to know that Ashley had died for her sins and was now resting in peace. I would tell her, too, that the chocolate chip cookies were a perfect hit.

Smoke Rings

Just as we were about to step onto the ice, Nonna nudged my arm away and opened the bank door. She slipped and her wig flew into a snowbank. "My back! My back!"

I yelled, "Help!" Tony, a kid from school, came running from the gas station. A crowd of about ten people surrounded us, mostly women. Tony tried to help Nonna get up, but she screeched, "My God. You're hurting me. Someone call an ambulance. I think I broke something. Don't anybody move me. I want a professional." Her coat was splayed open, and I was amazed that she had managed to create a rip in the leg of her pantsuit; there was even blood. Tears streamed down her cheeks.

The manager from the bank came outside. "Let me help you get up."

Nonna hollered at him, "Don't touch me! I slipped on ice. Who is your maintenance person? Must be a *bombast*. He should be fired." She moaned, the tears continuing, mascara a dirty mess on her cheeks.

"I've got your wig," a hunched-back elderly woman with an empathetic expression said. "Do you want to put it back on? I'll help you."

"Are you crazy?! What's a wig gonna do for me. What I need is an ambulance."

"Ma'am, I can assure you that an ambulance is on the way," the manager said. He reminded me of Cary Grant in his dark suit, white shirt, and tie. His wavy dark hair was parted on the side.

"I was only trying to help," the elderly woman said, handing the wig to a twenty-something lady with bright red lips and oversized tortoiseshell sunglasses. She looked disgusted, and passed the wig to a gray-haired short man to her left who twisted it with his hands.

"Hey, ya gonna ruin that thing. It was expensive. I bought it at Filene's. Stop tugging it, Mr."

"Oh, I'm sorry. Didn't even realize I was." He gave it to a fat prim and proper woman in a green dress. It was like a game of Hot Potato, I thought.

"It's okay. It's okay," Nonna said wiping tears away with her hands. They were stained with mascara. "My poor granddaughter." She pointed at me. "What a trauma to see her Nonna almost die. I'm sure she's gonna have emotional damage from this whole experience."

"Ma'am. She'll be fine. It was just a fall. It's not like you're dead," the manager said.

The prim lady blurted, "That was uncalled for. How insensitive." She looked to the others for approval.

"Thank you, lady. Don't forget he said that. You're my witness." Nonna whimpered.

"Of course not, dear." The woman smiled, happy to be important.

"Oh my God! I really coulda died. Smashed my head open or something. And that would have been poor Molly's last memory of me. My brain all over the ice." She crossed herself.

The lady with red lips and glasses sized me up, then glanced at Nonna. She smiled, looking smug.

"Jesus! My leg is bleeding," Nonna exclaimed, inspecting her torn pants. "I bet I'm just covered in bruises." She began to breath deeply. "Oh, oh, oh! I think I'm having agita!"

The gray-haired man said, "What should we do? What should we do?!"

"Take some deep slow breaths, ma'am." The manager kneeled beside her and tried to hold one of her hands. Nonna pulled it away.

"Who are you? So you think you're a doctor now?"

"I was trying to calm you." He noticed the mascara on his hands and wiped them on his pants.

"Keep your paws off me."

The ambulance arrived as if on cue, and the crowd opened to make way for two burly men who checked Nonna's vital signs and lifted her onto a stretcher. They were very sympathetic, and Nonna kept saying, "What nice boys." Once she was secured in the ambulance I entered and sat beside her. As we drove away, the siren sounded. Nonna placed her hand over her mouth to suppress laughter, smiling at me. I had to turn away because I knew I would laugh, too. "This is just awful. Just awful," she said to the young man on the other side of her stretcher.

"You'll be okay. We are going to take good care of you."

"Thank you, dear."

Through the back window of the ambulance, I watched the crowd disperse. The woman with the red lips remained for a few moments, staring as we drove away. She was smirking at me. I stuck my tongue out and smushed my face against the window, then I put on Nonna's wig.

When we arrived at the Emergency Ward of the Massachusetts General Hospital, the paramedics lifted her stretcher from the back of the ambulance and pushed through sliding doors that opened automatically. I followed them. We were greeted by a tall thin nurse with a white cap atop an immaculate blond bouffant. She put her hand on the stretcher and began asking the paramedics what happened. Nonna interrupted, saying she had a terrible fall on an area that should have been cleared of ice. A clerk at the receiving desk motioned for me to approach. He asked for Nonna's information—name, address, allergies, past medical history, doctor, etc. I gave him as much information as I knew, then was brought to an area in the back of the Emergency Ward, a large room full of stretchers partitioned with curtains. A lady with a bruised face and no teeth grinned at me from across the room. Nonna was staring at the ceiling from her stretcher when I reached her. She patted my hand on the railing of her stretcher when she saw me. "You did good."

After a while, the curtain was pulled back and we were greeted by a handsome muscular doctor in blue scrubs. He requested that I step away so he could examine her. He closed the curtain and I heard him ask a lot of questions. Nonna told the story of her fall again, this time embellishing details, saying how inconsiderate and cold the bank manager was to her. "I have witnesses."

The doctor listened patiently. He said that she was pretty bruised up with a small laceration on her thigh. She would probably feel worse a few days from now after the adrenaline rush had subsided, but he didn't think she had broken anything, and the laceration did not need stitches; it just needed to be cleaned up to prevent infection. He was going to order some X-rays just in case. Before he left, he asked if there was anyone he should call.

"There's no reason to bother my daughter or son-in-law. And I live with two nutso sisters who will just panic and give me a headache. Once I have the X-rays, and you give me the okay to go, my beautiful granddaughter will ride home with me in a cab."

"Okay, Mrs. Janssen."

"Don't call me that. Call me Agnella. Janseen is my married name. My husband died a long time ago. Julien was from Belgium. I'm an Italian. He was a crossdresser, you know. I should have stuck to an Italian. Never met an Italian crossdresser. Maybe it runs in Belgian families. What do you think?"

The doctor laughed. "I really don't know. I'm not sure what to say."

"Ah. What can you say? People have their ways. Caught him wearing my black panties and expensive red lipstick. He saw me in the bedroom doorway, then ran outta the house and drove away. Bam!" She clapped her hands. "The next thing ya know, he was hit by a train. Dead in an instant. Where he was going, I don't know. Was a real shame."

"Well, Agnella." He tried to change the subject. "Your granddaughter looks like a responsible young lady. I'm sure you will be taken care of." He pulled open the curtain and smiled at me. I loved his white teeth. He said I should stay with Nonna and pull the cord for the nurse if Nonna suddenly seemed drowsy or confused. Then he left, clipboard in hand, with a good story to tell his co-workers.

A young timid nurse cleaned out the laceration. We waited for the X-rays, which seemed interminable, but eventually Nonna was cleared to go. The whole affair had lasted about four hours. Our family probably assumed we were shopping and that we had stopped to eat lunch. The cab dropped us at Nonna's and we began to climb the stairs to her apartment. "Be quiet like a mouse," she said, pointing to the door of my aunts' apartment. "I don't want Aunt Helena and Aunt Bianca to bother me. They'd just blow things out of proportion and get hysterical."

She moved slowly up the stairs, stopping every now and then to rest. "That whole affair really knocked the wind out of me."

When we were seated in her living room, she took off the wig and laid it neatly on the coffee table. "Ya know, when I saw you put that thing on in the ambulance, I thought, God, how she looks like me when I was young. I'm an old lady now, no longer beautiful, but such is life."

"I think you're beautiful."

"Of course you should say that. I'm your grandmother."

After a few minutes of silence, when she seemed like she was going to nod off, she sat bolt upright, very alert. "Ouch!" She placed her right hand against her side. "I wish I hadn't fallen so hard." Then she said, "Molly, we gotta take pictures. We need evidence for a lawsuit. Let's go into my bedroom and check out the damages."

Nonna stripped completed naked, throwing the blue velvet pantsuit and her undergarments onto the bed. "Those clothes are going in the trash. Well, maybe not the bra and panties." She stared at herself in the mirror. For a moment it seemed she forgot I was there as she traced the bruises on her saggy body, turned and looked over her shoulder so she could inspect her back." Without looking at me, she said, "Grab the Polaroid from the left bottom drawer of my dresser."

I did so, and then she said, "These pictures are gonna be the icing on the cake." She laughed. "That's funny, 'icing.' Don't you think, Molly? I mean considering how it happened." She put her hands on my shoulders and stared into my eyes. I could smell her sweat, her oldness. "I know what you're thinking."

"What?"

"You're thinking your grandmother has sagging breasts, a sagging ass, and a flabby arms." She pulled the skin underneath her biceps and flapped it with her hand. "You don't want to get old, I know. But that's life. I had beautiful firm skin and was quite pretty like you, but aging is a terrible thing. You lose your looks, and then sometimes your mind. Or maybe you get a horrible disease. And there's nothing you can do about it. You just gotta carry on and get as much as you can out of every moment you are alive." She smiled, kissed my forehead, and pinched my cheek. "Now pretend you're a photographer for *Vogue* and snap some pictures."

It amazed me that she knew what I was thinking. Seeing her old body made me nauseous, afraid of the future.

"Look, this bruise looks like a cow." She pointed to the back of her right shoulder. "And this one over here on my ass cheek looks like a barn. What do you think?"

"I can see the cow, but I can't see the barn."

"Well maybe not a barn. Some sort of building though. I think it's the Vatican. I got the pope's house on my ass."

"I don't know what the Vatican looks like, Nonna."

She eased herself onto the bed and patted the area beside her. I sat down.

"It's a fancy schmancy palace where the pope lives." She moved my chin with her hand so that I was staring into her rheumy brown eyes. "Listen to what I tell you. What we did today, some people would consider wrong. Certainly the pope." She laughed. "Grab the cigarettes from the beside table, will you?" I reached over. "And the ashtray. . . Oh, and the lighter." I handed them to her. She placed the ashtray beside her, lit a cigarette, inhaled deeply, and blew smoke rings. "See those puffs of smoke." I watched them float in front of her face.

"Yes, Nonna."

"Look at that one over there in the corner," she pointed, "It's disappearing already. Here one minute, gone the next."

I watched the empty air. "So what?"

She slapped my face. My skin burnt and my eyes started to tear up. When I tried to move my hand to my cheek, she pushed it down and held it against my thigh.

I was crying. "Why did you do that?"

"Because you gotta be tough. You don't get anything in this world the easy way. What we did isn't going to hurt anybody. That big bank is gonna settle once we threaten a lawsuit."

I turned my head. I felt a pit in my stomach.

"Don't you look away!" She grabbed my face. As she spoke, I could feel her spittle on my nose. "And don't you dare utter a word to anyone about our plan today. You understand?"

"Yes," I mumbled.

"Say it louder."

"Yes! I won't say a word."

"Your poor Nonna and you were walking to the bank. I slipped on ice and had a bad fall." She laughed. "And I got bruises to prove it. She stood up and pointed to the Vatican. "As God is our witness."

I laughed and wiped tears off my cheeks.

"How much money do you think we'll make?"

She gazed at her body in the mirror above her dresser, as if making an appraisal. "I'd say about ten grand. Those hotshots at the bank won't want any bad press, especially about a poor old lady falling on ice." She stood up and moved the ashtray to the top of her dresser, then tamped out her cigarette. "Now you go downstairs and make us some coffee while I wash up and get dressed."

When I was in the kitchen, I heard her fall down the stairs. "Oh shit!" was the last thing she said. I found her body on the mahogany landing. There was a pool of blood around her head, and her right arm and left leg were contorted, like the Gumby doll of an angry child. I stepped over her body, walked up the stairs, and into her bedroom, where I sat down and lit a cigarette. I coughed a bit, but as I watched the smoke rings dissipate, I realized Nonna was right.

"Here one minute, gone the next," I said to myself. Then I walked to the phone on her bedside table and dialed 911. "My grandmother," I screamed. "She fell down the stairs and I think she's dead."

Myra Bocca

Just before the Shoppes of Wilton Manors, where Espresso Boys was located, Gabe and I passed a New Age bookstore called Sacred Ashes. We paused and looked in the window at a display of crystals and gemstones, silver and pewter jewelry, chalices, glass skulls, and crystal balls.

"Let's go in. Maybe they'll have some books on grieving," Gabe said. My aunt had just passed away. A male couple holding hands smiled at us as they passed. The warm breeze of the Florida evening felt good.

"I'm not grieving. I didn't like her much," I said quietly.

"Yes you are." He took my hand and pushed open the door. Enya was playing softly and there was an overpowering smell of sage. A woman wearing a bright pink muumuu embroidered with a design of blue, white, and orange tulips that rose from the hem like a garden, waved to us from the register at the back of the store. "Come in. Come in. It's so good to get a little business."

We passed a case with a wide variety of incense sticks (I assumed this is why the store was called Sacred Ashes), books, tarot cards, essential oils, prayer flags, greeting cards, postcards, photo frames, and several other new-agey items. The woman came out from behind her counter as we reached her. "I'm Myra. Myra Bocca." She had a large toothy smile, and her eyes—golden brown behind blue cat-eye glasses that were popular in the 50s and 60s—reminded me a bit of my Nonna's.

"I'm Gabe, and this is Molly."

She looked us over. "You're not a couple of course. He's too handsome to be straight." She waited for my response.

"I'm not a lesbian, if that's what you're thinking."

"Ya never know. A lot of lipstick lesbians in this town."

She pointed to the center of her forehead. "I'm a bit psychic. Both of you could be, too, if you rub this area right here." She put her hand against my forehead. "Feel the energy, Molly?"

"No."

"Well, I'm activating your forehead chakra. It's the main switch for the universal force, the awakened spirit, the center of higher consciousness."

I burst out laughing. "I don't believe any of that."

Myra frowned. "You will, dear, you will."

"Hey, are you from Massachusetts?" Gabe asked.

"Yes I am," she said. "See, Molly. Gabe's psychic. She gestured to all the items that surrounded us. "Already, the universal force is doing its thing."

"Not really," Gabe said. He lowered his head and smirked. "It was the way that you pronounced 'dear' that clued me in. You dropped the 'r.' "

"He's a smart one," she said, puckering her lips and raising her eyebrows, as she looked at me. She stared for a moment at my face. "What's wrong?"

"Nothing. Why do you say that?"

Gabe put his arm around my waist.

"No one fools Myra. Something is bothering you. Did someone die recently?"

"Lots of people experience death. That's not psychic," I said. Then to Gabe: "Let's go get that latte and dessert."

"You're avoiding the question."

"I don't really think it's any of your business, Myrtle."

"It's Myra . . . Okay, okay. I can tell you are upset. I just sense things is all." She moved behind the counter and began opening a box. "New inventory."

"Molly didn't mean to be rude," Gabe said. "She's just a private person."

I glared at him. "I can speak for myself, Gabe." He cocked his head back slightly.

"I *thought* there was a death." She crumpled up the torn brown paper from the package and tossed it in a wastebasket behind her, then lifted up the box. "Perfect timing," she said, repositioning her glasses and reading the box. "You know what this is?" Her voice was solemn as she looked into our faces.

"Apache Tear Tumblestones," I said. "Am I psychic, too?"

Myra laughed, glancing at Gabe and placing the box on the glass counter. "Oh, she's a tough one." Then she smiled at me. "I like you. You're headstrong and stubborn."

"And you're Italian," I said.

She turned around and saw that I was reading a sign that read, "The trouble with eating Italian Food is three days later, you're hungry again." Both Gabe and Myra laughed.

She nodded at the sign, then said, "Yes, Molly. I'm Italian just like you. I knew the minute you walked into this store. I said to myself, 'Now there's a strikingly beautiful Italian woman.' And I also said to myself, 'She doesn't look like she's married.' " She stared at me. "Why *aren't* you married?"

"Because I don't want to be," I said. "Men are a pain in the ass. Sorry, Gabe. And again, it's none of your business, Myrtle."

"Hey, I agree." He shrugged his shoulders and turned his palms upward.

"It's Myra. I have a feeling you're saying the wrong name on purpose. But that's okay. I've gotten under your skin. I tend to do that with a lot of people." She bent forward, placing her elbows on the counter, resting her head in her hands. "So speaking of food, why don't the three of us go to dinner sometime? My treat. You're obviously new to Wilton Manors. I'm a wealth of knowledge about the area and Florida itself. Everybody knows me. Just ask around. I could tell you stories. Whadaya say?" She smiled.

"Sure. Why not?" Gabe answered.

"And you, Molly? There's a nice old lady inside this muumuu. . . . What do you think by the way?" She lifted her elbows off the counter and twirled around. "I usually wear clothing that hugs my figure, but this thing is so comfortable." As she finished her whirl, she knocked the box towards me. I caught it.

"Oh, sorry about that. Good catch. Whew! I'm all out of breath. I gotta start working out. The problem is I'm too damn lazy and I like to eat." She slapped her backside and turned around. Looking over her shoulders she said, "Just look at the size of this toosh. There's a lot to grab onto, but in this town I'm outa luck."

"I'm sure there are a few straight men in Wilton Manors," I said.

"Yeah, a couple. I did have a fling with the Greek guy that owns the coffee shop you're going to. Espresso Boys, right? And I'm not gonna pretend that was my psychic ability. All the gay guys like that place. He's a nice guy, the owner I mean. Alexander Michaelis. Also from Massachusetts by the way. We used to get along. Had a little falling out. But that's a story for another night." She opened the box of Apache Tear stones and pulled one out.

"This is for you, Molly."

"I don't need it."

"It's good for healing grief. Please take it." I did.

"Made out of a type of Black Obsidian rock," she said. "Also good for grounding and protection. And keep it in your pocket near your genital chakra. Does wonders for your vagina, enhancing sexual energy."

"I think my vagina is in pretty good shape," I said, smiling. "But I'll use it for maintenance." I put the stone in my pocket.

"Of course it is. Not all saggy and dry like mine. Wait til your pubic hair turns gray. Depressing as hell." She grimaced, patting her pubic area unconsciously.

Gabe and Myra exchanged phone numbers before we left. Myra walked us to the door and gave us both a hug. "Welcome to Florida. Enjoy your evening."

After we passed her shop, Gabe said, "She's a character. I like her."

"I find her a bit intrusive. And you know how I feel about this higher power shit. The New Age Movement is just watered-down religion. I get pissed that people like Myra take advantage of the tragedies and insecurities of others."

"But maybe there are powers and mysteries to this universe beyond our ability to understand? I know we've had this discussion before." He smiled at me.

I laughed. "Yes, yes we have. And you're still trying to make a believer out of me."

We walked further down Wilton Drive. The street was bustling with gay men. An older man in a red Miata blared Christina Aguilera's "Beautiful." Every once in a while I spotted women, mostly lesbians. Palm trees along the street moved in the wind. I was living in a heterosexual wasteland. I ruminated about the strangeness of the experience with Myra, the coincidences: she reminded me a bit of Nonna—the color of her eyes and her dramatic flair, but not her overall look, and I suspected not as intelligent. Nonna was also more beautiful. Myra had a receding chin and a wrinkled prune face. The coincidences--that she was part Italian and from Massachusetts, her statement about the recent death, and her opening a box of supposed stones for grieving—were a bit weird. What were the chances of her opening a box of "grieving" stones at that moment? Maybe the black stones had nothing to do with grieving and she was making it all up, just a good reader of people, a con. In her business, you had to be.

Espresso Boys was busy. The slogan on the door read, "Where the coffee and men are robust." Several men, varying in age from twenty to fifty something, sprawled on the comfortable black leather sofa, loveseat, and chairs. When Gabe and I entered, most looked at us. Gabe, of course, garnered the most attention. His good looks were nice "eye candy," so I was told by his friend Walt. "He gets attention wherever he goes," Walt told me once. "Go for it, I tell him. Enjoy the deliciousness of sex."

A *Harry Potter* movie played on the four television screens. Most of the men looked bored, barely talking to one another, instead texting on their cell phones or chatting on a "dating" app called "ManDate." Occasionally, they flipped through gay rags called *Buzz* and *411*, mesmerized by the glossy ads of sexy men selling anything from plumbing services to legal work. There were even ads for doctors. Gabe once showed me an ad with a bare-chested hunky doctor wearing a stethoscope.

As we walked to the back counter to order our drinks, men continued to admire Gabe's beauty from the tables along the sidewall. I got passing glances, but women, I soon learned, were sometimes met with hostility in establishments that catered to gay men. Some of the men were kind, and a lot would comment on my good looks, makeup, and hair. If you were a pretty woman, you got attention, especially if you were an accessory to a gorgeous man like Gabe. The term that I sometimes heard mumbled in reference to me was "fag hag," which irked me.

A handsome older man with a full head of salt-and-pepper hair asked how he could help us. I looked at the desserts in the display case, none of which seemed too appealing.

"I'll have a large latte and one of those brownies." I pointed.

"And I'll have a cappuccino," Gabe said.

"No dessert?" the man said.

"No, I have to watch my waist." Gabe patted his perfect abdomen. I rolled my eyes.

"These young guys are crazy," the man said to me. "When I grew up, men didn't care about looking so good. The gay guys are just as vain as the women." He laughed.

I deduced that this was Mr. Michaelis, the gentleman Myra told us about.

"Well I'm a woman, and I don't worry about my looks." I smiled at him. "It's boring."

"That's cause you're lucky. You got those Mediterranean genes like me. What are you, Italian? Jewish?"

"Italian."

"Aahh. The Italian women are some of the most stunning." He laughed, making our drinks and talking over his shoulder. The latte machine whirred as he foamed the milk. "But Greek women aren't so bad either."

"You're Greek."

"How'd you guess?"

"I'm psychic."

He laughed. "Yeah, like that one up the street. The owner of Sacred Ashes."

"We just came from there."

He put our drinks on the counter, then placed my brownie on a small white plate with tongs. "Ahh. Myra. Don't trust a word she says." He had a tired dark complexion with deep wrinkles around his penetrating eyes, which were brown and thickly lashed. The sclera that surrounded his irises was very white, accentuating his perfectly capped teeth. He was handsome, even with sagging jowls, and I could see why Myra found him attractive.

"I hope you like the brownie. Not homemade, but I buy from good bakers." He handed me the plate. Gabe grabbed our drinks.

"Why shouldn't we trust her?" I said, before following Gabe to a table at the back.

"She's a lying greedy bitch. She'd sell her sister if she could."

"Does her sister live here?"

"Catherine lives up in Massachusetts. That's where Myra and I are from. The sister hates Myra. They haven't talked in years." He looked at the blond guy in line behind me. "Can I help you?" The guy started to answer, but Mr. Michaelis cut him off, calling to me as I walked away, "Enjoy your brownie. Stop by again if you want to get the dirt on her." He checked out my ass.

When I got to the table, Gabe said, "I think he likes you. Dirty old man."

"He's not that old. Late fifties." I looked back at him. He was busy making another drink. "And good-looking in a Robert DeNiro type of way."

"I thought you were finished with men?" Gabe broke off a piece of my brownie.

I sat up straight, brushed my fingers through my hair, and said. "It's always good to be open to change." A man with nice biceps at the next table smiled at me. By the front door, an intoxicated man entered, clutching the arm of his friend, who rolled his eyes and frowned.

"I won't argue with that." Gabe's eyes moved to the television screen on the opposite wall where *Harry Potter and the Chamber of Secrets* played. The character Ron was saying, "Do you think it's true? Do you think there really is a Chamber of Secrets?" to Hermione and Harry. While I watched the scene unfold, I thought how life was one great chamber of secrets and wondered how any of us could ever begin to know what was true.

I set the table and lit some candles. What I enjoyed most about living with Gabe was dinnertime and afterwards when we would sit together in the media area of the living room to enjoy news or a movie on the large-screen television.

"This is delicious," I said after my first spoonful of his risotto, a delicious blend of rice, asparagus, spices, and a creamy sauce.

"Here. Have some bread," he said, his mouth full, passing over the wooden server on which he has sliced a French baguette. I buttered a piece.

"Remember, my mother and her friend Evy are visiting this weekend. They arrive Saturday morning and leave on Monday, Columbus Day."

"Yes, I remember. I love your mother. She's so warm and funny. She doesn't even realize how hilarious she is. What's Evy like?"

"She's a great friend to my mother. A lady from Scotland with the best expressions. You'll love them. Kind, absolutely lovely. She's helped my mother a great deal over the years. When my mother was recovering from all those surgeries for her leg and back, Evy was a godsend. Of course, my sisters helped out, but they had to work. Evy was always there to assist."

He motioned for my wine glass and poured some more Chardonnay. "Oh, and we're going to dinner with Myra on Thursday evening. Is that okay?"

"Yes, I told you I want to be more social."

"She really likes us." Gabe scratched his chin and sipped some wine. "I can't figure it out."

I was silent.

"What are you thinking?" He smiled. "I know when you are holding back."

"Gabe, I don't want to say, because you will think I'm being a misanthrope once again, not giving people a chance."

"Oh, come on." He moved the fingers of his hand in the air towards himself. "Bring it on. What's your criticism?"

"She makes me uncomfortable. You know I can be guarded. I just find it funny that she has taken such a liking to us so soon. She doesn't even know us."

He laughed. "Maybe she truly is a psychic and knows that we will be great friends."

"I doubt it."

He paused the spoonful of food he was about to eat and stared at me.

"Gabe, I told you, I'm going. I gave you my word."

"It will be fun. Even if she turns out to be a nut and your suspicions are true. Consider it an adventure, as my mother would say."

"I will. Here's to adventures." I raised my wine glass. He did as well. "A toast to a future filled with good times and friends."

On any given weeknight at the Backyard Cafe, three waiters and a busboy move quickly to serve a crowd made up of pairs or groups of older gay men, some whose bleary red-rimmed eyes divulge a week, or even an afternoon, of drinking and partying (doing drugs). The diner, which opened as a Greek restaurant in the 1980s, had changed hands a few times through the years. At one point it was a Hungarian restaurant; the most recent incarnation occurred when the owner of Charlie's, the dinner club next door, purchased it. Since then the clientele has been mostly gay.

There are about 16 brown formica tables with aqua-green padded chairs. The walls of the place are painted gray-and-white faux marble on top, and fire-engine red on bottom. Black wainscoting above an 8-inch wallpaper design of dancing coca cola bottles and caps runs the perimeter of the oddly-shaped octagonal room. A counter above a base wall of shiny aluminum sheet metal, seats about 10 people along the north side of the restaurant. On the walls are black-and-white photographic prints of James Dean, Marilyn Monroe, Madonna, and Fred Astaire. Behind the cash register is a large close-up of Liza Minelli's face. The shabby drop-ceiling squares are painted steel gray to hide water stains, grease, and grime.

I took in all of this, after Sal, a balding forty-something bear-type with round brown eyes, rubbed Gabe's shoulders and took our drink orders. Myra was supposed to meet us here at 6:30. It was now 6:45.

"Do you think she forgot?" I asked.

"No. She'll be here." Gabe was reading the menu. "Have you decided what you're gong to order?" He pulled his menu back and looked at me.

"I'm going to have the Greek salad."

Sal brought our wine. "Who you waiting for?"

"Myra Bocca, the lady who runs the New Age shop across the street."

Sal rolled his eyes. "She's always late. Cheap as shit, too. Leaves 10 percent if I'm lucky. She can be entertaining though. Lots of the guys in town love her. They think she's *fabulous*." He laughed.

The door opened and in she walked. She was wearing tight jeans, a black v-neck t-shirt that showed off her cleavage, and what I call come-fuck-me pumps. I thought she looked ridiculous for her age. Her makeup was overdone, especially the bright orangey-red lipstick and oversprayed hair that topped her head like a cresting wave. I imagined a mini surfer riding her crown.

Gabe stood up. "Hi Myra. We're over here."

Sal retreated to the kitchen.

"Hey, aren't you gonna ask me what I want to drink?" Myra called after him.

"I'll be with you in a moment."

She sat down. An overpowering sickly sweet floral perfume surrounded us. I coughed.

"You getting sick, honey?" She put her hand on mine. I noticed a gaudy most-likely fake ruby ring and several age spots.

"No. Actually, it's your perfume. I think you put too much on."

Gabe smiled and pretended to read the menu.

"You want me to wash some off? I was so excited to meet you, I think I got carried away."

"Yes, I would appreciate your washing some off. Otherwise, I'll be coughing throughout the dinner. I have asthma."

"Sure. Sure. I'll be right back."

We both watched her waddle towards the rear of the restaurant. She tapped Sal on the shoulder and ordered her drink. He looked irritated.

"I didn't know you had asthma, Molly."

"I don't, but did you smell that shit? Makes me nauseous. It's like she's laid out and surrounded by flowers at a funeral home."

Gabe laughed. "What an image."

"Don't you think she's dressed a bit inappropriately for her age? Who wants to look at those sagging wrinkled breasts?"

"Trust me," he said. "No one in here is paying attention to her breasts."

"Is that better?" She asked when she returned.

"Much. Thank you, Myra." I handed her my menu. She looked around for Sal. "Where is that guy? He gives me the worst service. And I'm always so nice to him. Leave him the biggest tips."

Gabe and I looked at each other.

"Why don't you decide what you want to eat? I'll get his attention." Gabe signaled him.

Sal came to the table with a whiskey on the rocks. "Thank you, sweetie," she said, without looking up from the menu.

"Have you all decided what you want?" Sal said.

"I'm still making up my mind." She waved for him to go away and said, "Come back in a few minutes."

Eventually we ordered and the food was brought—my Greek salad, Gabe's turkey club, and Myra's meatloaf with extra gravy. Myra dominated the conversation. She wanted to tell us all about her life.

"I don't want you to get a wrong idea of me from all the stories you hear. A lot of liars and jealous types down here. Like Alexander."

"Who's Alexander?" Gabe said.

Myra wiped some gravy that had spilled in her cleavage. "Mr. Michaelis, you know, the one who owns the coffee shop."

"He's handsome," I said. "Seems very nice."

"He can be charming. But don't let those good looks beguile you. He likes to tell stories." Her eyes teared up.

"What's wrong?" Gabe said.

"It's just that I went through quite an ordeal before I moved here."

"What happened?" I wasn't buying it. She was a terrible actress.

"I'll tell you the God's truth." She held up her hand like a boyscout. "I was the wife of a very wealthy man. Lazarus Bocca. Have either of you ever heard of Bocca hats?"

I shook my head. Gabe said, "Yes. You mean those fedora hats that stars like Humphrey Bogart wore in *Casablanca?*"

"Exactly." She smiled at Gabe. Then she looked at me. "You know what he's talking about, Molly?"

"Well I know what a fedora is, but I've never been one for fashion. And I never watched *Casablanca*. I don't like that genre of film."

Myra opened her mouth and raised her eyebrows. I saw bits of meatloaf on her tongue. "My God. *Casablanca*'s a classic. What's the matter with you?"

I laughed. "I don't care if it's a classic. If I don't like something, I don't pursue it."

"Hmm. This one is quite opinionated." she said to Gabe. "I bet she can be a real bitch." She laughed.

"I bet you can be a bitch, too." I smiled at her.

She paused and looked at my hair. "You should consider a dye job. You're getting a few gray strands by your temples." She picked a bit of meatloaf off her lap and threw it on the floor. "I know a good hairdresser if you need a recommendation."

"I like my gray hair." I looked at her head. "Cheap dye jobs look awful."

Gabe eyed me. "Back to your story, Myra. I want to hear."

"Well, when Lazzy died."

"Lassie?" I said.

"Lazarus. My husband."

I laughed. "Sorry. I thought you said Lassie, but I guess you wouldn't have married a dog." I had finished a second glass of wine and could feel myself getting silly.

"My Lazzy was a beautiful man. Very handsome."

I burst out laughing, spitting some wine. "I'm sorry. That just sounded funny to me. I keep picturing that beautiful collie from the series. Now *that* was a classic."

Myra ignored me. "After Lazarus died." She looked at me. "My stepchildren--you see he was my third husband--they wanted to take the entire inheritance. We had set up a trust, Lazarus and I." Once more she looked at me. I pursed my lips so I wouldn't laugh, and I feigned interest. "And the deal with the trust was that everything would be dispersed evenly among his kids and mine from a previous marriage. His kids took me to court and I lost everything."

"How is that possible?" Gabe said.

She picked up a napkin and wiped her jeans. While looking down she said, "Well he had three children. Two girls and a boy. The boy was one of those vindictive fag types. Jimmy was . . . is his name. God, I wish he were dead."

Gabe's eyebrows lifted and his eyes widened.

"Oh, I got nothin' against gays, Gabe. I wouldn't be living here if I did." She laughed. "It's just that he was a big pain in the ass. Told me I was full of shit when I tried to explain my side of the story. All I ever wanted was for the trust to be settled fair and square. He was the ring leader in taking me to court." She paused. "And you know what the bitchy queen did to me?"

I took a sip of my third glass of wine. "I have no idea. Please tell me."

Gabe warned me with his eyes.

She moved close and placed a hand on each of our forearms. "He reported me to the IRS for tax evasion and fraud. I lost all control of the trust. Now I'm broke."

"I'm confused?" Gabe said. "Tax evasion for what?"

"I owned a little restaurant. Nothing fancy. Called the Sunnyside Café. My poor son. Worked so hard in construction, then he hurt his back and had to go out on disability. Well, I did what any loving mother would do. I let him work under the table at the Sunnyside. Those disability checks weren't nothing to live on."

"So you committed a felony," I said.

"Don't get attitudey with me, Molly. I'm opening my heart to you."

"Tell me how your son, who was collecting disability for a supposed back injury was healthy enough to work in a restaurant. Restaurant work is tough. Just look at how these waiters are running around." I motioned to Sal and the others.

"You would have done it, too, if you ever had a kid. Which I doubt you ever will if you keep spending all your time with gay men. But no matter." She looked at Gabe. "She's past her prime anyway. Few men will want her now, especially in this town." She laughed. "Just look around." She turned and looked at the crowd of men behind her.

"How the fuck do you know what I would have done in your situation, or if I'll ever have a child, Myra? You know nothing about me." I stood up. "I'm done." I opened my purse and threw my credit card on the table. "This meal is on me. I'm going to the ladies room. And then I'll meet you outside," I said to Gabe before moving my face close to Myra's. "I don't believe anything you say. That *fag* Jimmy was probably right."

The next day, Friday, I realized that my credit card was missing. I checked the dining room table when I got home from school to see if Gabe had put it there. When I did not see it, I looked on top of Gabe's dresser, where he threw his spare change, receipts, keys, etc. The card was not there either. I called him at the gym, where he worked as a trainer.

"Gabe, do you have my Visa card?"

"Let me check."

I heard weights clanking and Madonna singing "Tell me love isn't true. It's just something that we do" in the background.

"I checked my wallet. It's not there," he said.

"Do you think you could have left it at the Backyard?" I asked.

"Sorry, Molly. I can't remember. I might have. Honestly, I just wanted to get out of there after that scene with Myra. Why don't you call them?"

I called the restaurant. The guy on the other end of the phone told me to hold while he checked. He put the phone down and I heard snippets of conversation. Someone said, "Be careful crossing the street."

The host picked up the phone. "Sorry, Ms. It's not here. Give me your phone number and I'll call if anyone turns it in."

I did and thanked him. Then I called the credit card company. As a way to verify my identity, the woman asked about recent charges. I told her that the last charge would be for dinner at the Backyard Café.

"I see some others here from 9:15 this morning."

"What?"

"Well there's a charge for a Samsung forty inch LCD television from Sears."

"I didn't buy that."

"Hold on. There's a couple other charges."

"Some DVDs from a website called the Adult Boutique. *Debbie Does Dallas, Feeding Frenzy 3: Swallow the Leader,* and *Private Fetish 4 Pack.*" The woman had a monotone Texan accent.

I burst out laughing. "I didn't order those either."

"Hmm . . . There are also bulk orders of incense supplies from someplace called The Witch's Garden. Did you order those?"

"No." I felt my anger rising. "But I know who the witch is."

"Huh?"

"Never mind. It's obvious my credit card was stolen. The only legitimate charge is from the restaurant. The others aren't mine. Can you cancel the card?"

"Of course, Ms. Bonamici."

"Will I have to pay for the other charges?"

"No, ma'am. Obviously you have been the victim of fraud. Your account has fraud protection. I will erase the other charges and forward you a new card through the mail. In the meantime, I'd contact any businesses that might have your credit card on file. . . .While I have you on the phone, would you like to hear about our rental car collision policy or accidental death and dismemberment insurance?"

"Not right now, but thank you."

When I hung up, I called Gabe again.

"The bitch stole my card."

"Myra?"

"She charged a television and some pornographic DVDs."

"Molly, that could have been anyone in this town."

"How many gay guys order incense in bulk from a place called the Witch's Garden and a pornographic movie entitled *Debbie Does Dallas*?"

He was silent.

"Gabe?"

"Molly, don't do anything rash. We will talk about what to do when I get home. You did cancel the credit card, right?"

I told him I did, then hung up. My impulse was to drive to Sacred Ashes and confront Myra, but I knew I had to calm myself and wait for Gabe. I poured a glass of wine, sat on the patio, listened to bird calls, the click of the bamboo stalks moving against each other in the wind, and the sound of water falling on pebbles at the base of the fountain.

After dinner, Gabe and I decided we would talk with Myra at the shop the next day. She opened at noon on Saturdays and Sundays. He said I was too angry to do anything that night. And besides, the card was canceled, so no more charges could be made.

His mother and her friend Evy were arriving tomorrow. We figured the two would be hungry after the plane ride so Gabe called Mrs. Callaghan and gave her directions to the Backyard Café across the street from Sacred Ashes, where we would meet them around 12:30, after our talk with Myra.

Saturday morning I took a quick shower, threw on my usual outfit, jeans and a black t-shirt, and headed to Espresso Boys. I told Gabe, who was sleeping late after a night at the bars, that I was going for coffee but would be back around 11 am so we could go together to Myra's place. When I opened his bedroom door, he was sprawled out naked, twisted in his sheets. "Okay," he mumbled.

I knew Mr. Michaelis opened his coffee shop at 9 am. I wanted to get there before the place was too crowded. He had mentioned that he knew Myra's history and I wanted his opinion about what had happened.

When I entered, he was explaining to a cute little blond guy how to make the cinnamon buns. There were only two customers in the shop—a tall thin black guy with high cheekbones and deep-set animated eyes, and what appeared to be a lover or a very close friend, a handsome Robert Redford lookalike, who kept saying, "too much fun" as they watched a black-and-white film on the large television. I looked at the screen.

"It's *All about Eve.*" The black guy smiled at me.

Bette Davis had just said, "Everybody has a heart—except some people."

"Great movie." I smiled and walked to the counter.

"Mr. Michaelis, do you have a few moments to talk?" The blond guy looked up from the cinnamon rolls, where he was squeezing the glaze from a piping bag. He appeared a bit panicked.

"Sure."

Michaelis said to the guy, "Don't worry. It's slow now. Won't pick up for an hour or so when the guys start dragging themselves in hungover, desperate for coffee. You're doing fine, Brian." He patted his shoulder, then came around the counter.

"Follow me."

We sat at one of the back tables by the counter with sugar and stirrers.

"You want a latte? Something to eat?"

"No. No. I don't want to take up your time. I know you're working."

He looked around. "Do I look busy?"

I laughed. "I guess not."

"Give me your hand. You look nervous"

His hand was warm.

"I'm a bit upset."

"What's wrong?" His face was concerned.

"Myra Bocca stole my credit card."

He slapped his other hand on the table and laughed. The blond guy looked over. "She's up to her old tricks."

"You said you knew her in Massachusetts. Do you mind if I ask you some questions?"

He shrugged his shoulders and lifted his arms in an a welcoming gesture.

"Did you date?"

"Molly, I know you're the type I can be perfectly frank with. . . I fucked her. We didn't date. Myra is a slut and, in addition," his face reddened at some memory, "she's one of the most evil people I ever met. She and I were part of a group that used to go drinking together. The two of us, her husband Lazarus, and another guy Joe. This is before Lazarus and she were married, by the way. I'm not the type of person who would sleep with another man's wife. I don't want you to get the wrong impression."

"I'm not judging."

"The guys and I would pick her up. One time she got in the car and said, 'I'm so fuckin' horny.' Now that's not something a woman says to guys unless she's asking for sex. She made the rounds with the three of us. We'd go out drinking, and take turns bringing her back to our place for the night. She loved it! Eventually, though, she showed more interest in Lazarus. I warned him. I said, 'She only wants your money.' You see, he was rich. Joe and I, we weren't poor, but we didn't have the fortune that Lazarus did. His family owned a hat company."

"This is what I don't get. Why would she steal my credit card when it's so obvious that I would find out?"

"Molly, you don't understand. Some people in this world are evil to the core and just don't give a shit. You ever hear of the term 'sociopath'?"

"Yes, of course."

"Myra is a sociopath. They do whatever they want. They don't think about the consequences. I read a couple books on the subject. I'm not a big reader, but after what she did to Lazarus, I had to understand. A friend of mine recommended an easy read, nothing too technical—*The Sociopath Next Door*. You should read it."

"Gabe and I went out to dinner with her the other night—that's when she stole my card. She told us that her stepchildren tried to screw her. Evidently, there was some trust that Lazarus and she had set up so that she, her children from a previous marriage, and the children of Lazarus would all be treated fairly when he died. Myra said the stepchildren wanted everything."

"That's a goddamn lie!" he said. Brian, the blond guy, looked over. Michaelis asked, "How are the buns?"

"My buns are fine. How are yours?"

Michaelis waved his hand at him and started laughing. "These gay guys crack me up. Make everything about sex."

"What's the real story about the trust, Mr. Michaelis?"

"Call me Alexander. . . By the way, she probably planned to steal your credit card or your money. Or to ingratiate herself to you so that she could use you in the future. That's how sociopaths work."

"Tell me the real story about her past."

"Those stepchildren—great people by the way—wanted nothing more than to settle the trust as it was designed. Myra went through five lawyers fighting them, claiming that all of Lazarus's assets belonged to her. Lazarus, he was a damn fine man, wanted everyone to be treated fairly. One of the best men I ever knew." His eyes filled up. "You should have seen the antics she pulled before he died."

"Like what?"

"Out of nowhere, after twenty years of marriage, she sent a sheriff to their house while she was at the restaurant. The guy handed Lazarus a deposition notice that she wanted a divorce. This after he treated her like a queen their whole marriage. Not only did he take care of her, but he took care of all her kids—bought them cars, gave them money, paid for schooling. As I said, he was a fine man—generous beyond measure."

"Why would she do something like that?"

"Cause she's rotten, Molly. She had the gall to tell one of the judges that she filed divorce simply because she wanted to find out how much money Lazarus had. Why not ask him directly? . . . She suspected Lazarus was hiding assets from her. Meanwhile, she contributed nothing financially in all the years they were married. . . . Lazarus was devastated. Those kids of his, they were fantastic. You could see how much they loved him. Took care of him to the end.

"And get this." He was getting agitated. "After she found out that he had lung cancer, she canceled the divorce, told one of the daughters who asked how he made out at his doctor's appointment that he was fine. The poor girl. She learned about the lung cancer after she called to check on a blood test for the Coumadin he was taking. The nurse told her that the doctor had sent Lazarus and Myra home with an MRI disc of his lung. Told him to make an appointment with a cancer doctor right away. And you know what Myra did?

"She lied to the daughter. Said Lazarus was in perfect health, and the nurse must have confused the patients. Then she tried to take him to Florida the day after the appointment. His kids—best kids anyone could ask for—put a stop to that. Well it was all downhill from then on."

The door opened and we looked up at three hungover guys. Brian behind the counter glanced at Michaelis. "Guy's not too bright. I better get back up there. You think he could handle a few customers. Nice young man, but slow. There's two other things I want to tell you about what she did, though." He waved to Brian, "I'll be right there." Then he took both my hands in his. "These things will let you know just how bad she is. She fired an old lady waitress whose husband was dying just before Christmas so she could give a job to one of her granddaughter's friends. Told all the customers the lady had dropped dead! And the most heinous thing— is that the right word?"

"Yes."

"The most heinous thing is that she went to his wake after she told the stepchildren she would go earlier to avoid any friction. You see, she planned it all out. Just wanted to torment them, play games. She plunked her ass right next to his coffin at the wake. What could his kids do? I tell you, they showed grace and poise. Lazarus would have been proud." He put a hand over his heart. "Halfway through the wake, when all the people were streaming through, offering their condolences, she pranced around the room, over-animated to get everyone's attention. I thought I was watching an episode from *I Love Lucy*. It was sick! She started taking down all the pictures of Lazarus just to cause a scene."

"Alexander, I can tell this is distressing you. Go back to work."

He took out a handkerchief and wiped sweat off his forehead. "She never made it out of there with the pictures. Lazarus's son, Jimmy, he bolted from the receiving line and grabbed the photographs from her hand." He laughed. "I thought I was witnessing a drone attack." Then a police officer buddy of one of the girls escorted her out.

"Wow. What a story."

"Yup. I still can't believe the things she did." He pointed his finger towards me as he walked away. "You watch out for her. You hear me. That bitch is capable of anything. And I mean *anything*."

"I will." I rose from the table and thanked him on my way out. The two guys at the front were still engrossed in *All About Eve*. "Fasten your seatbelts," Bette Davis said, "It's going to be a bumpy night."

On our way to Myra's shop, Gabe told me he had asked his police officer friend to meet us there.

We were turning onto Wilton Drive headed south. A couple of shirtless guys walked their dogs on the sidewalks. A guy on a bicycle, also shirtless, turned to look at one of the them and was almost hit by a car.

"Jesus, these guys are crazy," I said.

"Horny, Molly, they're all horny. Any chance they can get to show off their six-pack abs, they do. I think I see that guy over there at least four times a day." He took his hand off the wheel for a second and pointed. "I'm surprised the paws of his bulldog aren't raw."

"Ow." I cringed at the thought. "Poor dog. . . .There's your friend." We pulled into a spot in front of a hair salon a few doors down from Sacred Ashes, where a bulky fair-skinned police officer with red hair and a beard stood. He smiled when he saw us.

We got out of the car and greeted him. He was wearing dark sun glasses but took them off and shook my hand. "I'm Johnny. Gabe's told me all about you."

"Great to meet you and thank you for coming." I looked at

Gabe, who was wearing black sweatpants and a blue tanktop. I wished I had dressed lighter. The sun was hot as usual. I was perspiring and glad that I was wearing black. "Gabe, you never explained why you invited Johnny. We're not going to have her arrested, are we?" I looked at both their faces.

Johnny said, "Nah. Gabe just asked my advice. I suggested I'd tag along since I'm on duty today. Purely an intimidation tactic is all. To be honest, Molly, even if we did charge her with credit card fraud, the chances of her being arrested are slim. South Florida has one of the highest rates of fraud in the nation. The courts don't even prosecute unless it's a significant amount of money. I'm sure Myra is aware of this. I did a background check on her. She has a history of petty crimes—shoplifting, check forgery, a slew of parking tickets, and yes, other cases of fraud. She was charged a few times, but she hired good lawyers, and either had the charges dropped or was put on probation. No jail time. I'm sorry to say she knows just how far to go."

We were walking in the direction of her shop. Gabe pulled me toward him, under the awnings from the shop so that I was in the shade. My face was sweating from the combination of heat, anger, and anxiety.

"After you," Johnny said, opening the door of her shop. Myra was on her knees behind the counter in the back, arranging new-age trinkets. The door chimed when we entered so she stood up. When she saw Johnny, her face turned white.

"Can I help you, officer?" she said. "Hi Molly and Gabe. I had a great time the other night." She put on a fake smile and picked some lint off her yellow dress.

"Yes, as a matter of fact, you can. I'd like to ask you some questions about a credit card you might have used."

Her jaw quivered and she looked at me with hateful scorn. "Certainly, I'll be right with you." Then she bent down and grabbed something from the case, a piece of crystal, and threw it at me. Her aim was awful. It hit Johnny in the chest. He pulled his gun from the holster.

"Stand right there. Don't move."

"Go fuck yourself, you bastard. I hate cops." She ran past the three of us crashing into the merchandise. Her display of cards fell over. I caught one of them. "A stone has no uncertainty—Carl Jung," it read. The whole situation struck me as absurd. Johnny chased her out the door into the street. Gabe and I started laughing. I picked up the crystal wolf that she had thrown.

"I feel like I'm in a bad movie," Gabe said.

Then we heard the loud screech of a car braking and a dull thump. The both of us ran outside. Mrs. Callaghan and her friend Evy were getting out of a yellow Mustang convertible. A crowd had gathered. People from the Backyard Café streamed onto the sidewalk. Sal, the waiter, ran over with an emergency kit. I also noticed the two guys I had seen watching the movie at Espresso Boys earlier. The shirtless dog walkers were there, too. I pushed my way through the people. A white-haired man told me Myra had tripped and slid across the pavement before she was hit by the car, which dragged her along the street when her clothing got caught on the edge of the undercarriage. "As soon as the driver realized what happened, she backed up, thinking she had driven over the body."

Myra's head was turned to one side, blood streamed from her nostrils and mouth, creating a halo-shaped pool around her head. Her face was bruised and scraped, the skin from her nose had ripped off revealing the cartilage, and her eye was wide open, pupil dilated. Her dentures lay on the street, smeared with blood and phlegm. The shin from her left leg protruded at an angle, its jagged edge pointing towards the sun.

The bulldog ran towards her body and began gnawing on the bone. The owner dashed over and picked him up. The dog's paws, face, and fur were bloodied. The guy pulled a blue T-shirt with ARMANI printed on the front from the back of his shorts. He began wiping the blood off his dog, then vomited, splattering individuals among the crowd. People squealed in disgust.

Mrs. Callaghan used her cane to nudge people as she made her way to the body. "Move the hell out of the way," she shouted. "I'm a nurse. . . . Evy, put on gloves from that emergency kit." A skinny guy opened the kit on the hood of the car and assisted Evy as she pushed her trembling hands into the gloves. "I'd do the CPR myself, but I can't bend down. Too much metal in me. I'll probably break something or loosen a screw," Mrs. Callaghan said, "You gotta do chest compressions. I'll tell you how."

Johnny tried to guide the both of them away from Myra's body, but Mrs. Callaghan hollered. "We've got to do something until the paramedics arrive. Believe me, I know what I'm doing." Johnny gently persisted in trying to move her away. She tapped him with her purple cane. "Officer, I got this. Call the paramedics."

"I already have."

Mrs. Callaghan said, "Listen to me carefully, Evy. Place the palm of one of your hands on top of the other. Then push down on her sternum 30 times. Think 'Staying Alive.' "

"Of course I want her to live, Maureen!" She bent down. Her purple hat fell onto the street. A short fat guy picked it up.

"I mean the song," Maureen said.

"Are you crazy? How can you think of a song at a time like this?"

"No, I mean as you are doing chest compressions sing the song in your head. It will give you the correct rhythm."

"But I don't know the song!" She was doing the compressions. "Oh, *crikey,* Maureen. I don't think I can do this!" Her face was panicked.

"Stay calm, Evy. Of course you can," Mrs. Callaghan answered.

The crowd began to shout, "You can do it, Evy! You can do it, Evy!"

The tall black guy stepped forward and began to sing, "*Whether you're a brother or whether you're a mother you're stayin' alive, stayin' alive. Feel the city breakin' and everybody' shakin'. And we're stayin alive, stay'in alive. Ah, ha, ha, ha, stayin' alive. Ah, ha, ha, ha, stayin' alive!*"

The crowd joined in, "*Ah, ha, ha, ha, stayin' alive. Ah, ha, ha, ha, stayin' alive!*"

Evy pumped. Her gloves were bloody.

Johnny said to Gabe and me, "I've never seen anything like this."

"I can't believe this is really happening," Gabe said.

Sirens sounded in the distance. The crowd stepped back.

Evy screamed, "Oh *crikey,* I think she *snuffed* it!" Then she burst into tears.

Maureen walked over with her cane and put her arm around her. "You did your best." She led her to the curb, where Gabe, Johnny, and I stood. We watched the paramedics take over. Additional police cars showed up and a van with "Broward Sheriff's Traffic Homicide Unit" printed on its side.

We all told Evy she did a wonderful job, but she was unconsolable. "God, I'm *knackered,*" she said between sobs.

Mrs. Callaghan saw our confused look, "She means she's

exhausted."

Johnny had moved to speak with the police officers who were questioning members of the crowd. Then he came back and told us that Mrs. Callaghan and Evy needed to go to the station for questioning, but it wouldn't take long; the accident was obviously not their fault. They were going the speed limit, and he and members of the crowd could attest that Myra ran in front of the car without even looking. He explained that their car would need to be towed and inspected but they would most likely get it back by tomorrow. Gabe and I thanked Johnny for his help and led the women to our car. I caught a glimpse of Myra's body on the stretcher. The blanket had fallen off one side. Her left breast swung loose like a flap and her mouth was wide open and ripped at the corners. However dishonest she was, she didn't deserve to die that way. The finality saddened me, and reminded me of the certainty of death.

I thought of the quote from the card--"A stone has no uncertainty"--and was reminded of the Black Obsidian rock in my pocket. I tossed it towards the base of her stretcher and watched it roll past her body into the shadows of the crowd.

A Prayer for Home

Show me the way to go home
I'm tired and I want to go to bed
I had a little drink about an hour ago
And it's gone right to my head
Everywhere I roam
Over land or sea or foam
You can always hear me singing this song
Show me the way to go home.

Aunt Helena and Aunt Bianca entered the front door, the brisk air of October following them. Both held bags from Filene's Basement in downtown Boston, a favorite for those in search of bargains. They were laughing about something.

"What's so funny?" Nonna asked.

"We just saw Mrs. Muldoon," Aunt Helena said. "Poor thing was drunk as a skunk. She was walking the street aimlessly. Said she was looking for her husband Jim. We had to lead her home and get her settled." She hung their coats in the closet. "Then she told us that the Happy Garden Chinese Restaurant was sending pork fried rice and egg rolls to her house every night. She swears she never ordered the food. Mary said, 'I don't speak Chinese. How in the hell could I order from those chinks?' 'Can't understand anything they say to me, yet I get chink food delivered every day about 5 p.m.' "

"She must be having blackouts and forgetting that she ordered. Or she's imagining that they are delivering the food. Mary has squash rot," Nonna said.

"What's 'squash rot' ?" I asked.

"Means your brain is rotted from too much alcohol, Molly," Helena said. "When she drinks, Mary gets delusional and hallucinates."

Helena and Bianca plopped into the cushy velvet green chairs, placing their bags beside them. Aunt Bianca assumed her usual disposition, staring into space, frowning and saying nothing. Her red hair was a mess and her lipstick smeared. She looked like a sad Bozo the clown.

"What happened to Mrs. Muldoon's husband?" I asked.

Nonna said, "Long before you were born, Mr. Muldoon died from a massive heart attack. Poor Mary was fixing dinner in the kitchen. When she called him to the table, he didn't answer. She went into the living room, where he would listen to the radio and read the paper, and found him dead in his chair, the paper scattered at his feet. She hasn't been the same since. Just drinks away her sorrows."

"Oh," I answered. I couldn't comprehend what it would be like to find someone dead, especially a husband or a family member.

"Well, let's take a look at what you bought? Did you get that pretty dress you wanted, Bianca?" Nonna asked.

"No, some bitch must have found it in the pile where I hid it."

I excused myself, saying I had homework. Then I went to Nonna's bedroom where I would hang out until it was time to walk home to my parents, who were busy closing the restaurant until after 10:30 pm. Most of my evenings were spent with Nonna. She and my aunts watched Tom Brokaw on NBC News while I retreated to the bedroom and read.

Nonna thought it would be charitable of us to visit Mrs. Muldoon. I didn't like Mrs. Muldoon. On a Saturday evening, when I was bussing tables in the restaurant, I accidentally spilled marinara sauce on an ugly blue puff-sleeve dress that she was wearing. She called me a "clumsy oaf," and complained to my parents. I didn't argue with Nonna about visiting her, though. Nonna was not someone to disagree with.

We walked precariously up the steps of Mrs. Muldoon's front porch on a late afternoon in December, "Mrs. Muldoon will slip and fall on this snow." About two inches had fallen that morning. "Grab that shovel against the house and let's clear a path from her door down to the street."

It didn't take us long; the snow was light and airy. I shoveled while Nonna gave commands. As we were stomping our feet and about to ring the doorbell, the door opened. "Aren't you going to clean the curb, too?" Mrs. Muldoon said to me. "I like to walk on the street you know. The slobs next door never clear the sidewalk." She must have been watching us from her living room window the whole time.

"Of course she will," Nonna said, and then to me, "Molly, just finish up that little bit while I go inside with Mrs. Muldoon. Then come in." Mrs. Muldoon held the door as Nonna entered.

"You'll do a good job, won't ya?" Mrs. Muldoon said with a fake smile. "Not make a mess of it like you do sometimes at the restaurant."

Nonna chuckled, and when Mrs. Muldoon turned, mouthed, "She's drunk. Ignore her." She pinched her nose and grimaced.

As the door shut, I gave Mrs. Muldoon the finger. Even though she didn't see my gesture, it gave me pleasure. I shoveled the curb, making sure to leave just a bit of snow on the curb, hoping she might slip.

I found the two of them standing in the archway that led to the living room. Nonna was oohing and aahing over a silver aluminum Christmas tree with a color wheel.

"I love those red and green balls, and the see-through ones, too." Nonna said. "Isn't it pretty, Molly?"

"It's gorgeous." I wasn't that impressed.

"Well the damn thing ought to be. Paid a pretty penny for it. At Sears, ya know. The girl in the store, a pudgy midget, said it was a specialty item."

"Oh, a specialty," Nonna said, winking at me. "Well it's beautiful, Mary. Now why don't we go into the kitchen and enjoy some coffee while we eat the cookies I brought you."

"I don't know why they call it a specialty item. They've been around for years," I said.

"Well it's special to me," Mrs. Muldoon snapped. "Where are the cookies, Agnella? I could use something sweet to get rid of the bad taste in my mouth," she said, looking at me. We walked into the kitchen

"I wrapped a few up and put them in here." Nonna patted her black leather handbag.

"Well I would think you could give me more than a few. What are you? Cheap?"

Nonna laughed. "Mary, you got the diabetes to worry about."

"Was she really a midget?" I interjected.

Mrs. Muldoon looked irritated.

"She's asking about the salesgirl in the department store," Nonna said.

"I know what's she's asking, Agnella. Yes, Molly. Or a dwarf. I don't know what ya call them nowadays. But nice enough, she was. And quite knowledgeable. She told me the tree was made in some town in Wisconsin. Would be an heirloom in the future. I said to her, 'I don't care about any heirlooms, dear, and I don't care about the future. I haven't got a soul to leave it to.' And don't ya know, the midget said to me, 'I'm sorry.' I said, 'About what, darling?' And then she said, 'That you haven't got any children.' I laughed and told her not to worry. Children could be a pain in the arse. Isn't that right, Molly?"

Mrs. Muldoon almost slipped on the red-brick linoleum floor, but Nonna was able to grab her arm and steady her into a chair. The kitchen smelled like a pine tree. Nonna explained to me later that the smell was from all the gin that Mrs. Muldoon drank.

Nonna brewed coffee in the percolator, after opening cabinets and rummaging through the disorganized mess of her cupboards. Mrs. Muldoon was silent, her eyes dreamy, looking out the window above the sink.

"Mary, where's the sugar?" Nonna opened the bread box.

"Hey, it's not in there. Look on top of the refrigerator."

"Crazy place to put it," Nonna said, taking the yellow sugar bowl and placing it on the table.

"It's starting to snow again," I said, following Mrs. Muldoon's eyes. "Guess you'll have to find someone to shovel for you later on."

"It is, and isn't it pretty. Do they still make snowflake cutouts in school, Molly? I used to love Christmas time when I was a tot."

"Mrs. Muldoon, I'm a senior in high school. We don't do things like that. They make snowflakes in elementary school."

"What a shame." Mrs. Muldoon said. "People at every age should make snowflakes. That's a joy of Christmas. Don't you agree, Agnella?"

Nonna was pouring the coffee and arranging the anisette cookies on a plate. "Yes, Mary. Snowflakes should be appreciated at every age." She opened the refrigerator and sniffed the small carton of cream. Her nose crinkled. "Mary, the cream's gone bad." She poured it down the sink and ran hot water. "We'll just have to have our coffee black."

"Let's have a gin and tonic instead," Mrs. Muldoon said. "Molly, too. She's a *senior in high school* now," she said, over-enunciating and smirking. "Too old for snowflakes" She laughed.

"We're having coffee. No alcohol. Wouldn't go with the cookies," Nonna said.

"Snowflakes form in the Earth's atmosphere when cold water droplets freeze onto dust particles. Depending on temperature and air humidity, the ice crystals create myriad shapes. No two are alike," I said. "I think that's more wondrous than anything we could create with a scissors and white paper. I prefer the realness of nature."

Mrs. Muldoon laughed. "Aren't you a whippersnapper. And all those big words: *myriad* and *wondrous.*" She humphed.

Nonna set the coffee and small plate of cookies in the table center. "Molly's very smart. She got a perfect score on her SAT verbal and almost a perfect score on her math. She's in the 99th percentile. Her IQ is 148."

"Whatever that means," Mrs. Muldoon said. "What else do they teach you? Do they teach you to count your blessings? Do they teach you your catechisms? Do they teach you the Ten Commandments, the Our Father, and Hail Mary? Now those are valuable lessons." She picked up rosary beads and some laminated novenas that were on the table. "Faith is most important, Molly." She shook the beads. "I pray every night for the Holy Father's intention that the Catholic church reign forever."

"Yes, of course they teach us those things, Mrs. Muldoon. I attend Immaculate Conception. The sisters have to explain all that to us. But I'm not sure I believe in any of it."

"What do you mean?" Mrs. Muldoon said. "So sacrilegious. And at this time of year." She tsk-tsked. "Now there's a big word for you." She laughed and sipped her coffee, then glared at me. "You are not smarter than God, Molly." She placed her cup down firmly. A bit of the coffee spilled over the rim.

"I think that Molly is saying she's a free thinker," Nonna said.

"A free thinker? What a bunch of malarkey. I don't even know what it means."

"It means she makes up her own mind about what she believes

and doesn't necessarily listen to what people tell her. She's an independent young woman."

Mrs. Muldoon guffawed.

"Let's change the subject," Nonna said. "No need to be arguing. It's not the holiday spirit."

"I suppose you're right, Agnella," Mrs. Muldoon said, raising herself from the chair. "I've got to use the little girl's room anyway." Nonna helped her stand.

"I'm okay, Agnella. Stop being such a mother hen."

Nonna laughed. When Mrs. Muldoon left the kitchen, Nonna whispered to me, "Go into the living room and get me a few of those see-through balls on the tree. Hurry up."

I did just that, bringing her two translucent balls and one red one. "I like the red one," I whispered. Nonna wrapped them in napkins and stuffed them in her bag, which she clasped shut just as we heard the toilet flush down the hall.

When Mrs. Muldoon returned, she said, "I was just thinking about Vivian Vance. It's sad that she died. Oh, how she used to make me laugh."

"Who's Vivian Vance?" I said.

"Ethel Mertz. You know. From *I Love Lucy.* Now that was a funny show. And Lucille Ball. What a riot!" Nonna added.

"God bless the people who make us laugh," Mrs. Muldoon said.

"I'll second that," Nonna said.

"I wonder what a dead body looks like. I'd love to see one," I said.

"What an odd thing to desire." Mrs. Muldoon pursed her lips.

"And although it's sad that Vivian Vance died, I don't see why her death is any more tragic than the death of anyone else," I answered. "She's no more valuable then the rest of us. Do you know there's approximately 153,400 deaths per day, or a little more than 100 per minute? Just think of how many people died while we've been sitting here. We are all specks of dust floating in an enormous universe."

"Your granddaughter is getting too big for her britches. Imagine? 'Specks of dust.' I don't even know what she's talking about half the time. Wanting to see a dead body, too? Where does she come up with these things? Jesus, Mary, and Joseph!" She took a sip of coffee, then murmured "specks of dust, specks of dust" and looked out the window. The black bark of a tree cut through a gray square of sky.

Nonna looked out the window as well. "Don't mind her, Mary. She's just a thinker."

"I could tell her a few things to think about." Her things sounded like "tings," and her think sounded like "tink." I was going to correct her but Nonna said, "We should get going. The snow is falling. And Molly's got homework to do. Don't you, Molly?"

"Yes, Nonna. And I want to add some more ornaments to our Christmas tree so it can be just as beautiful as Mrs. Muldoon's."

"Yes, yes," Nonna said, rising from her seat. "It's a beautiful tree."

Mrs. Muldoon escorted us to the door, commenting some more about my poor attitude, and then as we walked home, Nonna said, "Such a shame. An old woman with all her money. Drinking herself to death." She stopped suddenly and turned to me. "You've got to learn to hold your tongue. You'll never get anywhere in this world if you don't know when to keep your mouth shut. Learn not to be so fresh."

When we hung the ornaments on our tree, Nonna said, "She won't notice them missing. And it's a shame not to have them appreciated. You think they're lovely, don't you, Molly?"

"Yes, Nonna."

Later, as I lay on Nonna's bed doing homework, I picked up the phone and called the local Chinese restaurant.

"This is Mrs. Muldoon," I said, "Send me over an order of pork fried rice, egg rolls, and add some beef broccoli this time. And you'll hurry it up, won't you? I'm so hungry I could eat a nun's arse through a convent gate."

"You can choose to be happy or you can choose to be sad. Aunt Bianca chooses to be sad. It's our personalities, our attitudes, that determine how everything turns out. So choose to be happy and everything will be good. Are you happy, Molly?" We were having hot cocoa and biscotti in Nonna's kitchen.

"I don't really know."

"How can you not know if you are happy?"

"Well, I'm not sure what happiness is? Everybody talks about it, but I don't think I feel it like other people. I'm not saying that I'm sad, so don't give me that strange look. I just think that I still have to find out what happiness is. Sometimes I don't feel anything at all."

Nonna put her hands on my shoulders. "Maybe you don't think

you are happy. But you can pretend. Look at Mrs. Muldoon. She has a broken heart, but most of the time she tries to stay upbeat."

"I think she's a bitch."

Nonna laughed. "Well she is." She took a sip of cocoa. "But her bitchiness keeps her sadness from taking over. You've got to be strong to tame a lion. And sadness is a lion."

Nonna poured some more cocoa into our mugs. "Just look at the difference between Mrs. Muldoon and your Aunt Bianca. Mrs. Muldoon tries to stay peppy, and Bianca just sits and sulks. She rarely talks, and when she does, it's usually to complain. Always wants something for nothing. Thinks that she's treated unfairly."

"Mrs. Muldoon is peppy because she's drunk all the time."

Nonna smiled. "Well, that's true."

"Why is Aunt Bianca so depressed?"

"I don't know." Nonna looked thoughtful for a moment.

"She's always been that way. Even as a little girl. Miserable." She tapped my knee. "Did I ever tell you how she once stole money from the collection basket during mass?"

"No." I leaned forward. "Did she get in trouble?"

"She did."

"Maria Cennamo. That was the girl's name. She told Father Paul, a scary old Irish priest with white hair and a fat red face."

I laughed. "I can't picture Aunt Bianca doing something like that? She seems so sluggish."

"She's a crafty one, Molly. She pretended to put change in the basket but instead pulled out a dollar bill, hiding it in the palm of her hand." Nonna sighed. "I hate to tell you this about your aunt." Nonna laughed. "No, I don't. I like gossiping with you."

"What did Father Paul do about her stealing?"

"Bianca was lucky. He could have reported her to the police, but underneath that frightening exterior was a kind man. Her punishment was to clean and polish the altar every week for six months."

"And you know what Bianca did to Maria Cennamo, the girl who snitched?"

"What?"

"She smacked her on the head with one of those small Bibles we all used to own." Nonna laughed. "Maria never dared look at her again."

"Well I'm glad she found some use for that thing."

Nonna gasped. "Molly, don't ever let anyone hear you talk like that about the Word of God."

"Nonna, you don't believe it's the *actual* word of God, do you?"

She laughed. "Of course I don't. But that's not the point. Most people do. And you gotta fit in. Do you hear me?" She stared into my eyes.

"Yes."

"Good," she said, settling back in her chair. "Because appearances matter. Most fools are too stupid to know what's really going on." She groaned.

"Are you upset at me?"

"Of course not. It's just my aching back." She took another sip of cocoa, then put her mug on the table with a thump. "Molly, life is a game. Some people win and some people lose. You gotta do what you gotta do so that you always win. People will call you names. They may call you a bad girl or a mean girl. But it's never bad or mean to get what you want. Don't let anyone hold you back. What one person sees as right, someone sees as wrong. It's all relative." She placed our empty mugs in the sink.

"Do you believe there is a God, Nonna?"

"Why are you asking me that?" She turned from the sink.

"The idea of God doesn't make sense to me."

"Molly, you make me laugh. You think too much."

"But do you?"

"Do I what?"

"Nonna, you know what I'm asking."

She sat down and crossed her arms. "No."

"I don't think I do either. There is no heaven. There is no God. I think when we die, we just rot and become dirt."

"Oh. You make it sound so depressing. Don't think about all that. Think about life."

"I am."

"Just agree about with others about certain things. Like church and God, and all those crazy saints. You can't tell most folks how you really feel. You and I aren't like other people. They don't understand our common sense way of looking at the world." She patted my arm. "In order to be successful, you sometimes have to keep your opinions private. I want you to go off to college in the fall and become someone important. Maybe you will be a doctor?"

"I'm not sure about that, Nonna."

"Why not! Whoever says women can only be nurses is a

chooch."

I laughed. "What's a *chooch*? I never heard you say that before."

"Like your father. A jackass!"

"I didn't say I *can't* be a doctor. I just haven't decided what I want to study."

"I understand. No rush. You have time. Now help me clean up a bit, and then you need to go home. Your mother, I'm surprised she hasn't called yet. She'll be worried sick. She's a nervous type. Not like you, Molly. You have nerves of steel." She smiled.

We cleaned up, then Nonna followed me down the hall to the front door. As I stood on the landing, she kissed and hugged me. "Goodnight, mia bambina." I descended the stairs, pad softly outside my aunts' apartment on the second floor, and walked into the frigid air.

It seemed that I was engulfed by believers in those days. The Italians and the Irish were obsessed with church, religion, and the pope. Nonna called me later that week and asked if I would help her take Mrs. Muldoon to a Faith Healer that Mrs. Muldoon had heard about on the radio. The woman had allegedly cured a young girl whose cancerous tumors miraculously disappeared, and an old arthritic man who could barely walk.

"Does Mrs. Muldoon have cancer?" I asked.

"No. She said she wants to see the woman as a precautionary measure."

"That's silly, Nonna."

"Of course it is. Mrs. Muldoon is crazy, but I can't refuse to help her. That wouldn't be nice."

"Why can't she go on her own?"

"Oh Molly. She can barely find her way to Broadway downtown to do her food shopping. How's she gonna manage a trip to the center of Boston. That's like asking her to travel to Africa."

I agreed and on the appointed day, one Saturday in May, Nonna and I drove in her Plymouth Fury to Mrs. Muldoon's house. The day was brilliant. Not a cloud in the sky, bright sun, just a few clumps of dirty snow left over from a freak storm the previous week. There were puddles all over, and small streams ran in the gutters along the street. The temperature was in the low 50's and things were melting: water dripped everywhere. A chunk of icicles fell from the railing as we stepped onto the porch. I saw Mrs. Muldoon seated through the sheer curtain in her living room. She reminded me of one of the fortune tellers behind some lacy fabric at Wonderland Amusement Park. She got up when she saw us and opened the door.

"Come in. Come in. But stomp your feet first. Don't bring any of that wetness in here."

The house stunk like mold and soured milk. The living room to the right had boxes with clothes and old shoes spilling out. The fancy Christmas tree was in parts in front of the fireplace, and the ornaments were in a pile on her dark brown couch.

"Mary, it stinks in here. And what is that mess in the living room?" Nonna said, pointing to the boxes.

"Oh, I'm going to have a garage sale if I get inspired. Or maybe just donate the things to the Salvation Army. I hear they pick up stuff, don't they?" She led us into the kitchen.

"I don't know. But what I do know is that the any clothes from those boxes will smell musty. I'm not sure anyone would want them unless you put the stuff through the laundry."

On her grey Formica table were several plates with leftover food—bits of toast, old bacon, half-eaten sandwiches. The trash basket to the right of her white porcelain sink was overflowing. I saw the evidence of my calls to the Chinese restaurant that had fallen between the sink counter and the basket—dirty Chinese take-out boxes with wire handles.

"We gotta get you a maid. What's going on with you, Mary? Why you let your house become such a pigsty?"

"I've been busy, Agnella."

"Doing what?!" We were standing in front of the sink, which had hardened comet in its basin.

"Oh, this and that. But never mind. Let me just grab my coat from the back hall and we'll get going. Molly, are you excited to be healed?" Her pretty blue eyes sparkled. I thought she must have been very attractive when she was younger. Such fair skin and perfect teeth, or were they dentures?

"I don't think I need to be healed. I'm healthy, Mrs. Muldoon."

"Darling, we all could use healing. Ya know it's not only physical healing," she said, putting her arms into her red wool coat sleeves. I liked the black fur collar. "It's spiritual healing as well."

I was surprised by her peppiness, and frankly, how happy she seemed. She was usually such a bitch to me. She seemed as excited as my girlfriends before a date.

I was about to say I didn't need spiritual healing, but Nonna, as if reading my mind, gave me a look that said, "Keep quiet." She had spoken with me several times about perceptions and how important it was to for me to foster interpersonal skills. She said that my directness was admirable, but others might interpret it as rudeness. I was surprised when she quoted Emily Dickinson, a writer I had been reading quite a bit of lately: "Tell the truth but tell it slant." She told me she had picked up my poetry book from one of her armchairs in the living room, and opened to one of the dog-eared pages.

It took about 25 minutes to get to Tremont Street in Boston, where the healer saw her clientele. Her business was on the street floor of a six-story building with a variety of ornate architectural features. At the very top was a mansard roof with dormer windows. The gray exterior was dirty with lines of black and green that had formed from rain that had probably pooled on the many outcroppings and ledges, then seeped down the face of the building. The parlor where "Lady Jane" cured people was underneath a printing company squeezed between a luggage store on the left and a jewelry store on the right.

We parked across from the building along the edge of the Boston Common. I could see a line that extended from the front of the building and around the corner to Court Street. Nonna's parallel parking was awful and Mary kept screaming that we were going to hit the car in front or behind. At last we were parked just across the street on the Boston Common side. We paused for a few moments in silence, the three of us taking in the sights around us. Two skid-row type old men on a bench, wearing derby hats and unkempt, mismatched suits shared a bottle wrapped in a paper bag. One of them pointed to something at the top of the building and I followed his finger to a flock of large black crows perched on a ledge underneath an overhang. The people waiting in line were pathetic looking. Mostly old ladies, a few men, some with canes or crutches; a young blonde girl in a wheelchair. It was a motley group, a range of ethnicities, all seemingly poor.

"You sure you want to go, Mary? These people look pitiful. I think they need curing more than any of us." It was true. We were wearing nice dresses and overcoats. I thought we would be out of place in that crowd.

"Of course I want to go. Remember you can't judge a book by its cover." Mrs. Muldoon pushed her door open and pulled herself into a standing position.

"Well all I can say is that this is one hell of a book." Nonna said. She and I followed Mrs. Muldoon's lead, who told us to hold hands.

When we crossed, Nonna cut in front of an Indian couple, explaining to them that I had leukemia "very bad" and the doctors gave me three months at most. "It's urgent that we see Lady Jane. You don't want the poor girl to die, do you? She's my granddaughter!"

Mrs. Muldoon whispered irritably, "That wasn't a nice thing to do."

The woman was beautiful with large very dark eyes; it was hard to discern her pupils from the brownness that surrounded them. She had a red dot between her beautifully shaped arched brows, which I later learned in an Intro to Religion class was called a Bindi or Kumkum, marking a spiritual center or chakra, placed there out of respect for an inner Guru, all of which I thought was bullshit. She wore a purple saree and a pink head scarf. Her short bespectacled husband had a flat nose with large blackheads; tufts of hair sprouted from his nostrils and ears. He was wearing a blue navy suit and I thought he might have met his wife here after work. They spoke for a few moments in Hindi, then stepped back and nodded for us to move in front. There were grumblings and complaints from those behind the couple.

"Hey, go to the end of a line like the rest of us. What makes you so special, ladies?" an Irish-looking guy with a broad red face and a skully cap said.

Nonna teared up. "My granddaughter is dying."

The man's face blanched, and he looked at me with a horrified expression. "Sorry, lady. Not a problem." I tried to appear sick. I started shaking a little and drooled, not sure what a leukemia patient's symptoms were. The Indian couple stepped further back. I managed to create a string of saliva that dropped like the thread of a spider's web hanging off the bottom of my chin.

We turned forward. Nonna put her arm around me, as if trying to keep me from fainting. Mrs. Muldoon looked upward at the gathering of crows, which had increased since I first noticed them.

Nonna followed her gaze. "I hope they don't shit on us," she said.

"Oh, but Agnella, it's good luck. Let them poop if they need to. I've got a handkerchief in my purse." The idea of birds pooping on my head was vile, but I refrained from making a wiseass comment.

Finally we were inside. The healing room, or parlor, or whatever you call it, had metal fold-up chairs along the sidewalls. Some of the armrests were rusty. I thought we might need a tetanus shot if we sat in them.

Lady Jane sat in a large throne-like chair on a platform at the back of the room. She couldn't have been more that 27 years old, bleach blond long hair, a pixie face with deep-set shiny green eyes. She was very petite. I thought she would have been a much older woman. I was surprised at her outfit: a tight-fitting black and white dress with a very high hemline. She was busty and had long satiny legs that ended in white ballerina slippers with a flower patter of red gemstones near her pink toes. Her white string shoelaces were untied.

"Well, she's not what I expected," Mrs. Muldoon whispered, and sighed. "She looks like a tart that's trying to make a few extra bucks from her other job in the Zone."

"What's the Zone?" I said.

"It's where all the hookers hang out, just around the corner. Perverts, pimps, drug dealers, and dirty bookstores," Nonna whispered.

The old man Lady Jane was waving her hands over with her eyes closed yelled "Hallelujah" and threw his crutches towards the chairs on each side of the line of people.

"Watchit!" an old blue-haired woman shouted. Her voice was low and she sounded like a man. "You almost hit me."

When it was our turn, Lady Jane said, "I take it you three are together." She had a fake British accent with a hint of a Georgia twang. Mrs. Muldoon seemed disappointed. "Yes, we are together."

"What can I do for you?" she said, looking at each one of our faces in turn.

"Well cure us," Nonna said, a little irritably. I could tell she was exasperated that we made the trip here.

"Yes, I know that, but you must tell me what ails you."

"For Christ's sake, at our age, everything ails us," Nonna said, "Where do you want me to start. How 'bout you make my tits perky like yours?"

Lady Jane feigned indignity, but I saw right through her, and Nonna could as well.

"Agnella, you mustn't talk like that to this woman," Mrs.

Muldoon said. "I would like to be cured spiritually. Forget about my body. That's too far gone. I want my soul to be cleansed." Mrs. Muldoon was hoping for the remote chance that Lady Jane might be legitimate.

Lady Jane put her hands in a crisscross on Mrs. Muldoon's heart area, then closed her eyes, while she softly murmured an ostensibly sacred language. I thought I heard what sounded like 'pussy' in her gobbledygook. I think Nonna heard it, too, because she gave me a look at that moment and rolled her eyes.

"The masters have told be you are spiritually cured for your trip."

"Cut the crap! Mary's not going on any trip."

"That's not true, Agnella. I am," Mrs. Muldoon said excitely, as if there might be some authenticity to Lady Jane after all.

"Where the hell are you going?"

"I'm going home." Mrs. Muldoon was beaming.

"To your family in Ireland?" Nonna asked.

"Yes, to my family."

"And how can I cure you, little girl?" Lady Jane said, looking earnestly into my face.

"I don't know."

Again she did the crisscross thing with her hands. Again she murmured her sacred prayer. And again I heard a distinct "pussy."

When she opened her eyes, her face blanched. "What is your name?"

"Molly."

"Molly, I hate to tell people things like this." Now she was speaking in a mostly Georgia twang. "But I see gruesome deaths in your future."

"Let's get out of here," Nonna said, clearly upset. She started muttering in Italian.

"You are going to witness several deaths in your lifetime."

"Who doesn't witness death? We all die." Nonna said.

"No, Molly's situation is different," Lady Jane said, speaking to Nonna as if I weren't there. "I take it you are the grandmother."

"Yes. That's easy enough to tell. I couldn't be her mother. Too old and dried up."

"You are very good to Molly. You mean more to her than her own mother."

It was eerie how this woman knew that. "Okay," I said matter-of-factly. "Tell me about these deaths."

"You have the unlucky fortune of being someone who will either find dead people or be near them when they die in violent situations. I guess you might say, 'You're an Angel of Death.' " And then she started giggling like a little girl. It seemed out of her control and she curled up with laughter.

The Indian couple behind us hurriedly said something to one another and rushed out the door. In retrospect, I wonder if the woman's inner Guru told her to get the hell out of there.

"Angel of Death! *Ffangul'*!" Nonna said. She pulled Mary and me out of the line and we followed the couple. As the door shut, I looked back and saw that Lady Jane was still laughing. She waved to me. I mouthed, "Fuck you," echoing Nonna's sentiment.

During the ride home Mrs. Muldoon and Nonna argued over what "Angel of Death" might mean.

"Maybe she'll be a police officer," Mrs. Muldoon said. "That's a nice profession. Protecting the citizens. And all police officers witness death now and again, don't you think?"

"Are you crazy? No granddaughter of mine is going to be a police officer. I think that broad saw that Molly was gonna be a doctor." She smiled at me in the rearview mirror. "What do you think she meant, Molly? Or maybe a murderer?" She laughed.

Mrs. Muldoon said, "That's an awful thing to say."

"I think she was just making things up to frighten us," I said. "Maybe she spotted someone who would actually pay her further down the line, and she was in a hurry to get us out of there."

"The man on the radio said she doesn't accept any money. Believes she has a calling is what he said she said," Mrs. Muldoon answered.

"He said, she said? Do you know what Mary's talking about?" The car swerved as Nonna turned to look at me.

"Lady Jane. . . Watch it, Agnella!"

"I noticed people slipping her bills," I said.

Nonna zipped through a red light.

"Jesus, Mary, and Joseph! You're going to get us arrested," Mrs. Muldoon said.

"Then it's a good thing we have a cop in the back seat. She'll use her connections and get us off the hook."

We all laughed.

As we were passing a section where you could see planes from

Logan Airport, Nonna asked Mrs. Muldoon, "When is your flight?"

"What flight?"

"The flight to Ireland. When are you going home?"

"Oh . . ." She paused to think a bit. "I'm going the third week of August." I thought it funny that her pronunciation sounded like "turd."

"Well, at least we have you for a few more months. I'm gonna miss you, Mary. But I'm sure you'll be happier. Everybody needs family. And you got nobody here, right?"

"Nobody."

I leaned back in the seat and thought how Mrs. Muldoon and I shared something in common. Sure, I had Nonna, but I still felt very alone. But aren't we all essentially alone? A psychiatrist told me years later that each human being is limited by his consciousness. All lived realities are filtered through our individual prisms, he said. He added that we die alone as well, no matter how many people are around us. His words reminded me something the writer once Hunter S. Thompson once said: "We are all alone, born alone, die alone, and—in spite of True Romance magazines—we shall all someday look back on our lives and see that, in spite of company, we were alone the whole way."

Nonna paid for my graduation celebration in June at our restaurant eponymously named "Bonamici's," which means, by the way, "good friends." I have always found our surname ironic because my father was an unhappy person who rarely smiled and always stressed about the business. The fact that I had no siblings was a blessing, as it lessened my parents' financial burden. If I had siblings, I think the restaurant would have gone under.

Thankfully, I received an acceptance letter from Boston University at the end of April, informing me that I was granted a full four-year scholarship, so my parents did not have the worry about paying for my college education.

My anxiety-ridden mother stood at the hostess stand and greeted my extended family, mostly relatives on my father's side—aunts, uncles, and cousins. My father wanted to keep the event a family affair, so I couldn't invite any friends, not that there was anyone in particular I wanted there. Mrs. Muldoon was present, as well as Jimmy Scarfone, Nonna's friend, with whom I think she was romantically involved. When she talked about him her eyes sparkled, and one time on her kitchen counter I found some silverware that she had stolen from Jimmy's Harborside Restaurant. When I asked her about the cutlery, she explained she took them for Mr. Scarfone because they bore the imprint "Jimmy's" and thought it would be nice to give the pieces to him for his birthday.

Our family restaurant served the typical Italian dishes—entrees with veal, chicken, and seafood, as well as traditional Italian favorites, such as meat lasagna, baked ziti, manicotti, spaghetti with meatballs. The food was mediocre; this fact, my mother's nervous disposition, and my father's surliness contributed to the so-so revenue. Part of the working class, my parents were always struggling to get by, especially during my last year at home.

I was happy that my high school years were behind me, and I made a mental effort to remember the scene around me that day— the groups of people talking under the dim swag lamps with amber globes, the red and white checkered cloths on the tables, the maroon vinyl booths with cracks, the small tables with chairs, and the large mural of a canal in Venice. As a little girl I would stare at the gondolier with his white shirt and black pants, escorting a pair of lovers among the beautiful pink and white buildings. What was he thinking? Was he angry because he had to paddle all day for rich tourists? I imagined him whacking the heads of the couple with his oar and pushing them overboard.

"Molly!" Nonna yelled from an area in front of the stone hearth, "Come over here."

There was a din in the room--people chatting, busboys and waitresses setting up tables in the front with a variety of dishes. As I made my way through the crowd, several people said congratulations, *complimenti* or *buono fortuna*.

"You know Mr. Scarfone," Nonna said, pointing next to her with her glass of whiskey.

"Yes. Hi, Mr. Scarfone. Thank you for coming."

"I wouldn't miss it for the world. Nonna says you're gonna make lots of money. Says you're a very smart young lady."

I laughed. "I hope so."

"I was telling him the story about that *troia* from the Combat Zone. What was her name again?" I was surprised that Nonna was already drunk. "Lady something or other." She was slurring her words.

"Jane. Lady Jane."

"No lady calls Nonna's granddaughter an 'angel of death," Mr.

Scarfone said with simulated anger.

"If anyone is an angel of death, it's Jimmy here," Nonna said, laughing, choking on some of her whiskey, which spilled onto her black dress as she coughed and bent over. There were rumors that Mr. Scarfone was associated in some way with the Mafia.

"Gimme that." Mr. Scarfone took the glass from her hand and placed it on the mantel above the hearth. "Are you okay?"

"Of course I'm okay," she said in between coughs, "It went down the wrong pipe." When she had regained composure, she said, "I'll take that now," pointing to the whiskey glass.

Mr. Scarfone returned it and said, "Agnella, maybe you better slow down. You don't want to get stewed like that one by the window." He nodded towards Mrs. Muldoon.

My father came over. "Agnella, are you okay?"

"Of course, I'm okay. My Molly is graduating and going on to bigger and better things. Something you never managed to do, Lorenzo."

"Did you think about what Anna asked you?"

"Yup. And the answer is no, no, no! If you had managed the restaurant wisely, listened to some of my advice over the years, you wouldn't be in the state you're in. And you wouldn't have to ask your wife's mother for money."

Mr Scarfone raised his eyebrows at me.

"Well, the state *you're* in is pretty bad. You're drunk. And I don't need your goddamn help."

"Good. If you want to find a source of money, why don't you ask Mary over there." Nonna pointed to Mrs. Muldoon at her table by the windows. An empty glass was positioned at the table's edge, and she was drinking what looked like a gin and tonic.

"She's going back to Ireland in August. Loaded though. So you better hurry, Lorenzo. " She turned to Mr. Scarfone. "You should see the stack of cash she keeps in her breadbox. I bet she has money hidden all over her house. She hasn't been right since her husband died. If you ask me, she was lucky to get rid of him. I'd be happy with all that cash."

"Of course, you would, Agnella," Mr. Scarfone laughed.

"You're a cheap woman, Agnella," Dad said." His volume was raised and bits of spit flew from his mouth. "You won't even help your own daughter."

"Don't call me cheap, you son of a bitch. And Anna has nothing to do with this. It's *you* I won't help." Nonna dropped her glass. "Now look what you made me do." She glanced at the red tile floor. One of the busboys came over to clean up the mess.

"Hey, you two need to cool it," Mr. Scarfone said. "This isn't the time for arguments. Molly has just graduated. Today is *her* day."

"It's okay. I'm used to Italian dramatics," I shrugged my shoulders.

"Sorry, Molly," Dad said and walked away. If he were a dog, his tail would have been between his legs.

When he left, Nonna said, "Ungrateful man. But enough about him." She once again looked towards Mrs. Muldoon, who also appeared a bit tipsy. "Ya know, I don't know what in hell remains in her house. Every day that I drive by men are removing more furniture. She says she's donating her things to goodwill."

Mr. Scarfone looked in Mrs. Muldoon's direction. "How much money we talking, Agnella?" He twisted a ring on his left pinky.

"Jimmy, I don't know. Lots. Like I said, I'm sure she's got it stashed all over her house. Mary doesn't trust banks. Her husband was well to do. An electrical engineer. Created a patent for something to do with transistor radios. And she is pretty cheap. She'd let the roof cave in on her house before spending a dime to fix it up; it's a shit hole." She patted my arm and pushed me forward. "Molly, go talk to her. She looks lonely."

As I started to leave, Mr. Scarfone put his hands firmly on my shoulders and looked into my eyes. I noticed that his large gold ring had at least ten circular inlaid diamonds. "If you ever need anything, and I mean anything," he said almost menacingly, "call me."

"Thank you, Mr. Scarfone. I will."

When I sat down across from Mrs. Muldoon, she smiled and seemed genuinely excited. She used to be so bitchy, but the last few times I'd seen her, she had changed dramatically. She actually seemed to like me.

"Darling, it's a pleasure to see you. And aren't you as pretty as movie star. You remind me of Audrey Hepburn. You know her, don't you, dear?" She was wearing a bright yellow dress with a matching round hat. The color complimented her shiny blue eyes.

"I loved her movie *Breakfast at Tiffany's,*" I said.

"And wasn't that song so pretty? 'Moon River.' Oh, I'd sing a bit of it for you now, Molly. Ya know, I used to sing once."

"Really?"

"Yes, darling. That was how I met my husband. I played piano and sang at a nightclub in the Back Bay on Beacon Street." She looked out the window. Someone was parking a Dodge Charger across the street. Then she started to sing very softly, as if forgetting I was there. "Moon river, wider than a mile, I'm crossing you in style some day/Oh dream maker, you heart breaker/Wherever you're going, I'm going your way." Then she paused. "Oh, I'm a silly old lady. Too romantic, I think. Always been so." She leaned in a bit. "Are you romantic, Molly?"

"I'm not sure."

"Well do you have dreams, sweetheart?"

"Yes."

"Well good." She took a sip of her gin and tonic. " 'Your feet will take you where your heart is.' That's an old Irish proverb. Remember it."

"Sort of like your going back to Ireland?"

"Huh?" She looked confused.

"You're going home, Mrs. Muldoon."

"Yes, I suppose it is. I'm following my heart." She smiled. "And you must follow yours, too." She put a warm hand atop one of mine. "You and me. We're both starting a new journey. Like the rest of the song, and she began again, alternating between a faint croon and a whisper " 'Two drifters off to see the world/There's such a lot of world to see/We're after the same rainbow's end/Waiting 'round the bend, my huckleberry friend/Moon river and me.' "

"That was pretty," and I thought it truly was.

"Now get me another drink, won't you?" She gulped the last bit from her glass. "My huckleberry friend." She laughed.

I brought Mrs. Muldoon her drink. My mother called me to the center table where she and Dad sat. Dad pulled out the chair for me. Soon flute glasses of champagne were distributed to all. Dad stood up and clinked his glass with a spoon to get everyone's attention. Aunt Bianca nudged Aunt Helena, who was busy fussing over the arrangement of food on the buffet tables.

"I'd like to give a toast to my beautiful daughter, Molly," he said. When the room was quiet, he continued, looking directly at me, "Molly, you are a very intelligent girl. I don't know where you got your smarts from, but it certainly wasn't from your mother or me."

"From me," Nonna called out and people laughed. My mother looked embarrassed, smiled at me and squeezed my hand.

Dad answered her. "Not so sure. How smart is it to hang out with that shady character next to you?" Mr. Scarfone laughed, brushing a hand under his chin and flicking it forward. Many of the guests chuckled. Aunt Bianca looked at Mr. Scarfone, annoyed, humorless as always.

"Molly," he continued, "Your mother and I are very proud of what you have accomplished in school. And we are certain that you will continue to do even better in college and beyond. Here goes," he said, pulling a paper from an inside pocked of his black jacket.

Nonna called out, "Look who's smart now. You gotta read from a paper." Again there was laughter in the room.

My mother handed Dad his glasses from the table and he began reading, "Remember this, Molly: 'If you're going to lie, lie for a friend. If you're going to steal, steal a heart. If you're going to cheat, cheat death. And if you're going to drink, drink with me. *Complimente dottore!*"

"Bravo!" people shouted and there was clinking all around.

"Stand up, Molly," my mother whispered.

I stood and everyone clapped.

"Now *Mangia!*" Dad said.

Aunt Helena escorted me to the front of the buffet line, and others followed. Dad went into the kitchen to check on things. When my mother and I had returned to our table, she said, "I have something I want to give you. It ain't much, but I hope you like it."

"I'm sure I'll like it, Mom."

She reached down and took out a gold and yellow wrapped gift from a bag by her seat, placing it in front of me. Her hands were shaking.

"Open it," she said.

I removed the ribbon that she had wrapped around the sides of the present and meticulously looped into a floral pattern bow at the top, After I tore the paper open, I saw a black leather Bible with gold "Holy Bible" on the cover.

"It was the Bible I was given as a little girl by my grandmother."

"Thank you," I said, disappointed. I was hoping for jewelry.

As if sensing my disappointment, she said, "I know you read books. So many books." She laughed. "And I wanted you to have the most important book of all."

I pretended to smile. She said, "Open it."

In small cursive, she had written a list of chapter and verse numbers in black ink on the chafed red paper lining inside the cover.

"Those are my favorite parts," she said. "Promise me that someday you will read them, and think of me when you do. It will make me happy." Her large brown eyes were teary, but she was smiling, too. I thought she looked so tired; the olive skin on her gaunt cheeks was yellow. Her blue dress was loose, and she seemed to have lost weight.

"Of course I will, Mom." And many years later, after she was long dead and gone, I did.

Towards the middle of August, Nonna called me to say we were taking Mrs. Muldoon to the beach on August 15th.

"Why August 15th?" I asked.

"She says she wants to spend some time at the water before she goes home. And she requested that you come as well. Something about a cure in the water. Evidently it is the Feast of the Blessed Mother's Assumption into Heaven and because of that the salt water has a cure in it. I don't really understand it all, but Mary is adamant about going, and she wants both you and I to take her."

"Is she sick?"

"Not that I know of."

"Then why does she need a cure?"

Nonna laughed. "Maybe she thinks it's you and me that need the cure, and it is her final parting gift."

"Why would we need a cure?"

"Molly, stop asking so many questions. How the hell am I supposed to know what goes on in Mary's mind? Maybe she thinks we have sick souls."

I laughed. "Nonna, I don't have a sick soul, and neither do you."

"You can never be sure. Listen, consider it insurance. If there is something to this whole cure thing, maybe we get something good out of it. And if there isn't, so be it. The point is that she asked us to take her. And I'm not going to deny an old lady a last request of a friend before she goes back home to Ireland."

I agreed to go, and on the appointed day, a Saturday, Nonna and I picked Mrs. Muldoon up at her house. She was seated in a rusted orange chair on her front porch, one of her last pieces of furniture. She had donated practically all of it to charity, except for a few pieces of in her living room, kitchen, and of course, her bedroom. Her house was on the market, but she was lackadaisical about selling it, leaving it in the hands of a realtor downtown. She said she didn't really care when or if it got sold, which I found very strange. But what did I know about such things. I was a young girl with my eyes set on college.

Nonna parked in front and honked. Mrs. Muldoon was asleep. She was wearing what appeared to be a housedress, mostly white, with a spattering of red dots, and hideous black boots.

"What the hell is she wearing?" Nonna got out of the car and walked carefully up the rotting wooden gray steps. Then windows were rolled down so I could hear their conversation. When she was beside Mrs. Muldoon, she shook her. For a moment, I thought she might be dead.

"Mary! Wake up."

She woke, a confused look on her face, Her amber hair was a sweaty mess. The cast of the sun highlighted a matted ring that circled her hair, as though she had been wearing a hat earlier.

Nonna said, "What's the matter with you? Did you forget we were going to the beach?" She looked down at Mary's feet, tsk-tsking at a pair of black rubber boots. "You look foolish in those things. How you gonna get the Blessed Mother's cure if you don't get wet."

"Agnella," she said, rising at last, "There's awful rocks before you get to the sandy part of the beach, and my feet are sore enough. Don't you worry. I'm going to take them off once we settle in a good spot. I may even strip naked. Wouldn't that be a sight to behold?" She laughed. Nonna did, too.

"And where is your bathing suit?"

"Underneath my housedress, of course. You certainly didn't expect me to sit here like some *tool* in my swimsuit. What would the neighbors think? And that strange boy next door Dominic is always lurking about snapping pictures with his camera. Scared the bejesus out of me one evening last summer. Saw him peering in my living room window."

"He's a little slow, Mary. Good he has a hobby."

"Don't mind he has a hobby. Just don't want it to be me. Imagine him taking a picture of me sitting here in my bathing suit. God only knows what he'd do with it. Wank off maybe. Shoot his tadpoles at the moon."

I laughed at the imagery. Nonna looked at me, raising her hands in the air.

"Just last week he was going through my rubbish. Rang the door and asked if I was throwing out any 'good stuff.' Had the nerve to tell me he needed money and wanted to sell 'the stuff' that I didn't want. I hate that word 'stuff.' Don't you, Agnella? Children need to speak better English."

"Forget about him. Let's get going."

Nonna helped her down the steps, which creaked and almost seemed to cave in at one point, then guided her into the passenger seat.

"I'm delighted you could come, Molly," she said turning around. "It's a celebration for both of us, a baptism of sorts, as we begin our new lives." I realized that the red spots on her gown were tiny roses. "You must be looking forward to your studies. You have always been such a smart one."

"Very smart," Nonna interrupted. "Skipped a grade in school and tested genius on the I.Q. scale. Takes after me." She laughed.

"Yes, yes, I know. You tell me all the time, Agnella. What's most important is Molly's soul."

"I'm happy to go with you to the beach, Mrs. Muldoon," I said. I wasn't. I hated the beach, still do. The hot sun and sand, crowds of people, radios blaring, the smell of baby oil, jellyfish in the water. Although I did admire the sharks because of their single-mindedness, the way they hunted for prey. And sometimes I would hope to see one of the annoying boys get bitten, but the chances of that happening were slim

We parked on the beach side across from the Renwod Dining Room, a place Nonna had taken me to a few times. Mary was right about the stones. They did hurt your feet. The beach was packed with people and it was hard to navigate through the crowd, especially as Mary was a little tipsy. I realized she had been drinking because I had to turn the window down on the way over. She stunk of sweat and gin. Radios blared, children created sand castles, groups of ladies gossiped, and the sun was so hot. Finally we found a spot to put our blanket and fold-up chairs. Most of the women wore full-piece swimsuits, and many had housedresses like Mary. Three girls about my age ran out of the water as their little brothers splashed them with water from behind. To our right, a man dressed in pants and a shirt, which I could never understand at the beach, fixed the chain on his overturned bicycle. I wished we had an umbrella. I had to use the palm of my hand to shade my eyes from the sun.

When we were settled, I asked Mrs. Muldoon about the cure in the water. She sat between Nonna and I in our spot close to the ocean.

"Well, darling, today is when Catholics celebrate the Blessed Mother's Assumption into heaven."

"I don't understand."

Nonna rubbed baby oil on her arms, legs, and face, then lay down, uninterested in our conversation.

"What don't you understand?"

"The Assumption part. What does that mean?"

"Well she was raised into heaven three days after her death."

"What do you mean *raised*? She just flew up into the air?" I laughed.

"Well, I think so, Molly. Yes."

"How is that possible?"

"Darling, you've got to have faith."

"But it doesn't make sense. How can somebody just fly up into the sky?"

"I don't know, Molly. Don't think too much about it. Just believe it."

"I don't believe it. It sounds ridiculous."

Nonna sat up and gave me the eye, warning me not to press the issue.

Mrs. Muldoon pulled off her boots, then stood and took off her housedress. Underneath was a stylish black-and-white full-piece swimsuit. I never noticed what a round hard belly she had. She almost looked pregnant. For a second, I imagined she was going to demonstrate the assumption and fly up into the sky.

"Well, suit yourself. I don't question these things." She walked into the water. I watched her plod through the waves, then dive into the water and swim out a bit.

"Now Molly, how many times do I have to tell you not to ask so many questions? It's rude. Most people aren't like you." Her eyes followed Mary who was now a ways out. "The world is made up mostly lemmings and sheep. You have the good fortune, or maybe the bad fortune," she smiled at me, "of being a lion in a world of lemmings." She put her warm hand on my leg. "Who gives a damn if Mary flew up into the sky or not? Maybe that's what happened a few thousand years ago, though I doubt it." She turned and looked at the

95

man tending to his bike, then whispered to me, "I wish God would reach down and pull that one off the beach. Can't stand the sound of him moving that peddle and chain, and his hands are a greasy mess." We both laughed. A woman walked by with a white shawl over her head and a long white robe. She reminded me of a bride.

"Do you miss your husband, Nonna?"

"Here we go again." She laughed. "You ask the strangest things."

"Well, do you?"

"Of course not. Men are a pain in the ass."

"What about Mr. Scarfone?"

She waved her hand. "Oh, he's just a good fuck."

"Nonna!"

She whacked me playfully with the bag of fruit and nice Italian bread she had brought. "Well it's true. And you should see the size of his *cazzone.*" She moved her palms apart to give me an idea of the size.

"His calzone?"

"No." She laughed. "*Cazzone,*" emphasizing the "z" sound.

"Maybe that's why they call a calzone a calzone. It looks like a penis." She lay back down. "Look that up someday in one of your fancy college books."

"Nonna, I don't think my college textbooks will have that information."

"Then what the hell good are they?"

We both laughed. She closed her eyes and patted the blanket around her to straighten it out.

After a while, Nonna fell asleep. Mrs. Muldoon had stopped swimming and was standing, like so many of the people. But unlike so many others, who were chatting with one another in pairs and groups, Mrs. Muldoon looked towards the horizon; a rainbow had formed above a group of clouds. I was wondering if she was thinking about her journey home. Seagulls cawed, children laughed or screamed with sportive delight. I was sweating, so I got up and decided to go for a walk towards the end of the beach that was less crowded, near a fishing jetty, and several clumps of large rocks. I explored the spaces in between the rocks, looking for a lonely starfish, a shiny stone, or a clam with a secreted pearl, and unearthed small crabs in the sand. At one point I startled a mourning dove that sped from its cleft into the bright sky. It made a whistling sound as it rose and flew off; then descended over the water where Nonna was now standing alongside Mrs. Muldoon in the ocean. The waves glimmered like sparks from an unquenchable fire. On the jetty, a father and his son cast fishing lines into the sea.

Suddenly, Nonna and Mrs. Muldoon fell, surprised by spirited breaker that razed them in its wake. I ran to help, but delighted, too, in the spectacle—Nonna and Mrs. Muldoon seated on their asses, just a few feet from where the waves trickled to their end. In an instant they were kneeling forward, laughing so hard that they cried. I helped lift them, Nonna and Mrs. Muldoon, groaning in between guffaws, complaining that the soles of their feet were cramping from shells and stones beneath them. Every time I lifted them another wave splashed over us, and they fell back down, laughing even harder.

Mrs. Muldoon said, "My permanent is all ruined," while she fussed with her hair.

Nonna said, "Well, it didn't look so good to begin with, Mary," and they laughed.

Then Mrs. Muldoon reached for me, "Now raise me up in quickly, Molly, before the next wave."

I did so, all the while mesmerized by the wet silvery scalp that shown through her hair. I resisted the urge to touch the crown of her head. At last she rose from the sea.

"Molly, you're an angel," she said, when she was standing.

"What about me?" Nonna said, another wave splashing over her. "*Maron'!* Pull me up, Molly. If I get hit by another wave, I'm gonna curse the water. Thought this was supposed to be a blessing. More like a tidal wave if you ask me." With that, another wave splashed over her, and both Mrs. Muldoon and I pulled her up.

Later we moved towards the quiet end of the beach. We sat in the shade of a bony cliff, eating panettone, bananas, apples, and delicious cherries drenched in brandy. Nonna pulled baby-sized jars of Grappa out her purse. I draped a necklace of dried seaweed upon Mrs. Muldoon, and told her it was my version of a Hawaiian lei, a wreath presented ceremoniously to people who were coming or going.

"In that case, you need one, too," Mrs. Muldoon said.

"What about me? I could use a good lei," Nonna said, smirking.

I found two more pieces of seaweed and Mrs. Muldoon hung them on us. Her fingers were icy cold, like those of a corpse. I shuddered as they touched my warm skin.

The three of us made a toast to new beginnings, and we talked about the future until the sun began to set.

We were still hungry as we left the beach so we crossed the street and enjoyed a nice meal at the Renwood Diner. I had the seafood platter and Nonna and Mrs. Muldoon had sea scallops with pancetta, mushrooms, and fresh tomato. Nonna and I devoured our meals but Mrs. Muldoon couldn't finish her meal and asked the waitress to put the leftovers in a bag to go.

Mrs. Muldoon made a joke about this being our last supper. "Well, it is in a way, don't you think? I won't be seeing either of you again after tonight."

"Of course you will. You're not leaving until five days from now." Nonna said, motioning for the check. "I'll drop by before your flight on Thursday if I don't see you before then."

The waitress put Mrs. Muldoon's white doggie bag and the check on the table.

"Let me pay for that," Mrs. Muldoon said. "I appreciate you girls bringing me to the ocean today. I feel refreshed and healed. And you made me very happy."

"Well I'm glad that you feel good, Mary, but I insist on paying." Nonna took cash out of her purse and placed it on the bill. The waitress picked it up.

"I'll see you one more time, Mrs. Muldoon. Nonna's driving me to Boston University to speak with a counselor next Thursday. On the way over, we can both say goodbye."

"That would be nice, Molly." She smiled at me, then pointed at the faded beige and blue pattern of fish swimming above clamshells and starfish on the ocean floor. "I always loved the fish in this wallpaper. This one here looks like he's coming right towards us."

"I wish there were some shark," I said.

Nonna laughed. "Of course you would."

"Did you know that a fish is the symbol of Christ?" Mrs. Muldoon said, sipping her last bit of wine.

Nonna spoke while she finished a roll. "No, I didn't. Where'd you hear that, Mary?"

"Oh, I don't recall, Agnella."

The waitress put Nonna's change on the table. "Well, I'm tired. I don't know about the both of you. Let's get outta here."

We dropped Mrs. Muldoon off and she waved from the front

porch once before she'd opened the door. I noticed several trash bags along the gray clapboard wall.

"Wonder what's in all those bags?" I said, as we drove away.

"Junk. When you get old you accumulate a lot of useless things, Molly. And then you become one of them. So live while you can."

I noticed a white paper bag at my feet. "Nonna, Mrs. Muldoon forgot her leftovers."

"Ahh. Don't worry about it. Leftovers are another useless thing." Stone-faced and preoccupied, she stared into the dusk. The streetlights turned on. I looked out the passenger window. Two of the neighborhood boys waved from the sidewalk.

Nonna dropped me in front of my house, but I didn't feel like going inside. I felt distracted and uncomfortable but I did not know why, so I went for a walk. Perhaps it was Nonna's comment about people becoming "useless things" as they got older. Later that night I fell asleep thinking about the meaning of those words and living "while you can." I dreamt of seagulls pecking someone's eyes out, sharks in bloody water, and a singing red fish with white stripes along its sides. Dreams are so strange. I tried to remember what the fish was singing about. I couldn't recall the words, but the feeling that lingered was one of emptiness, an emotion I often felt.

Nonna had tried to call Mary on Wednesday evening to find out the time of her flight back to Ireland, but the phone service had already been disconnected, so we drove over around 8:00 am on Thursday morning.

"She may have already left." Nonna pulled the car into Mary's driveway. "But we might as well see if she's still here. I forgot to tell you, but when we were in the ladies room at the restaurant, Mary told me she had a gift for you. She said she left it on the table just inside the archway to her living room."

We got out of the car and walked up the steps. Nonna held her nose. "Those bags smell God awful. Maybe she dumped food from her refrigerator into one of them."

I rang the doorbell. We waited a few moments, then Nonna turned the door knob. When the door opened a horrible smell gushed at us--a combination of shit, vomit, body odor, and rotting fish, stronger than you can imagine, unless you've experienced it. A few flies buzzed in the air around our heads. As we turned into the living room, I noticed a small wrapped gift next to a white bag on the table. Nonna bent over and started vomiting.

I walked towards Mrs. Muldoon's corpse. She was seated in the purple chair that Nonna hated so much, eyes half open and bulging, tongue protruding. There was an intricate pattern of blood vessels and blisters on her face. She wore the same housedress from our day at the beach. It was smeared with blood dripping from her nose and mouth. Her face, arms, and legs were bloated; her abdomen was distended. Her skin was green, purple and black. White lines crisscrossed areas of red on her calves. There were two shimmering pools of urine on the mahogany floor at each side of the chair, as well as feces on the seat cushion.

I kneeled down and pressed my finger against a dark purple spot above her right ankle; the skin was so cold. The flesh broke and blood trickled slowly down the side of her enlarged foot. I stood up, then crouched to stare into the small slivers of her eyes. The pupils were fixed and dilated. The corners of her eyes were filmy and I thought I saw wetness along the sides of her nose and cheeks. Were they tears or simply the body's fluids seeping out? I touched her pretty red hair and some it fell to the floor in clumps. A bloody maggot emerged from her right ear.

I heard Nonna gagging behind me. She kept saying, "We gotta call the police." I couldn't look back and though I found the smell overpowering and coughed a bit, I drew closer. I guess you could say I was mesmerized.

"Molly! What are you doing? Call the cops! I'm too weak to get up."

I picked up the black-and-white photograph from the t.v. table and examined it: an attractive couple, the young Mrs. Muldoon and her husband, in their wedding attire. Both of them dressed completely in white. He wore a white tuxedo with a bow tie and a wing-tipped collar. On the top of her auburn hair sat a veil with a crest of small white flowers; there was a pearl necklace around her neck and both of them were smiling above a large bouquet of white roses that obscured parts of their chests. In the dark background, blurred white faces hovered like disembodied heads.

"Molly!!"

I turned the photo over. In blue cursive Mrs. Muldoon had written "August 15th, 1954. The happiest day of my life." Next to where the photograph had lain was an empty pill bottle. I pulled it close to read the label "Diazepam, 5 mg. tab. Take one tablet twice a day as needed."

Nonna had managed to make a phone call. I heard her in the hall talking to the police. "Hurry," she said. She hung up the phone.

"What the hell are you doing?" she screamed at me. "Get away from her."

I turned, accidentally stepping on one of Mrs. Muldoon's bare feet. The skin cracked; a clear fluid oozed from her big toe and the nail ripped off, falling like an autumn leaf onto the floor.

Then I walked over to the small purple box with my name on it. Inside was a gold necklace with an emerald and diamond cross.

Nonna stared at me. "What is it, Molly?"

"A useless thing."

A short while later, two patrol officers showed up. The older one, a man with steel-gray hair, Paul Newman eyes, and thick black glasses took Nonna and me into Mrs. Muldoon's kitchen to ask a few questions, while the young officer, clearly a newbie by the pale and frightened look on his pudgy face, stayed in the living room. He was probably in his early twenties. I overheard him calling his supervisor to report the scene. His voice was high and agitated. I thought he wouldn't last long in this profession.

When we were seated, the older policeman introduced himself as Officer Donnelly. "My partner is Officer Connolly."

I laughed because their names rhymed, and he gave me a strange look.

Nonna was staring blankly into the air, obviously in a state of shock. She was perspiring. I handed her a napkin from the table. She dabbed her face robotically.

Officer Donnelly gave up on asking her questions because she muttered an incoherent mix of Italian and English. He turned his attention on me, notebook and pen in hand. He asked for our full names, which I gave him.

"Does Mrs. Muldoon have any relatives we should contact, Molly?"

"No."

His forehead rose and he examined my face, scrutinizing me. "No one? No one that you know of, you mean?"

"No. I mean 'no one.' She had a husband but he's dead. Your partner will figure that out, though, when he sees the picture on the t.v. table in front of her corpse."

"What do you mean, Molly?"

I explained my curiosity about dead bodies and gave him the

details of what I had done, the writing on the back of the photograph.

"You touched the body?" I noticed a hint of anger or was it disbelief, maybe even revulsion? He moved uncomfortably in the chair.

"Yes. And the skin broke so easily. Does skin always break like that when you touch a dead body?"

"Well it depends how long it has been since the moment of passing." He stared at me. His eyes were light, so pretty, almost feminine.

"Passing where?" I teased him.

"To heaven, Molly." He pulled his chair back a bit and rotated his left shoulder to stretch. He pulled himself upward, puffing his chest. I noticed sweat on his face, too, and handed him one of Mrs. Muldoon's napkins. They were white with blue and white doves.

"How could you do that?" Nonna exploded. She stood and began wringing her hands. Then she fingered the cross around her neck.

I answered Officer Donnelly. "I don't believe she *passed* to heaven, sir."

"Molly, I don't much care what you believe. What else did you touch?" He spoke calmly, as if dealing with a lunatic.

"I touched her hair, and some of it fell out. You'll find it on the floor in a puddle of urine. There was a maggot in her ear."

Nonna ran to the bathroom.

"A maggot?"

"Yes, Officer Donnelly. As in a fly."

"That didn't bother you?"

"No." I laughed. "A maggot is just a baby fly."

I could hear Nonna retching down the hall. The toilet flushed. She entered with a wet cloth on her forehead and sat down.

"I'm sorry, Officer Connolly. This whole thing has been very upsetting," she said. I noticed for the first time the deepness of the wrinkles by her eyes. Her olive skin looked papery, like crepe. A blue vein in her temple bulged slightly.

"Officer *Donnelly,* ma'am. . . .It's quite understandable that you are upset."

"Huh?"

"My partner's name is Officer Connolly. I'm Officer Donnelly."

"Oh. That's right. Sorry."

"The sergeant has notified the homicide unit and EMS. They are on their way." Officer Connolly said, entering the kitchen. His eyes moved from Nonna to me.

"How's the girl?" he asked Officer Donnelly, as if I weren't present.

"I'm fine. Thank you," thinking, "better than you." His skin was a yellow pea-green.

"Sorry that you had to walk in on this, Ms. . . ." He looked at Officer Donnelly.

"Her name's Molly. Molly Bonamici."

"Ahh. Your last name means 'good friends' "

"You know Italian?"

"Yeah. Some of my best buddies are Italian."

"Mrs. Muldoon was Irish like you. I liked her in the end. I guess you could say she was one of my buddies."

"I see," he answered, raising his eyebrows at Officer Donnelly.

"Why don't you take Mrs. Janssen and Molly to the patrol car. Have them sit there a while."

A crowd had gathered. The blue light on top of the car cut through the air, highlighting faces like a strobe light. I saw Aunt Helena; Aunt Bianca stood behind her with one hand on Aunt Helena's shoulder. She looked like she was clasping a life raft, adrift at sea. I waved to them and smiled as we were ushered into the car. My mother and father were there as well. They tried to approach the car, but Officer Connolly said something to them and they moved back. My mother's eyes pleaded. She was excited as she talked to him, more animated than I had ever seen her. I guess they wanted to keep Nonna and me isolated.

"Well, she got what she wanted," I said inside the car.

"What are you talking about, Molly?! She's dead. Mary is dead."

"But Nonna, she took those pills on August 15, the anniversary of her marriage. She wanted to die on that day. Now it all makes sense. I think it's kind of sweet and perfect."

"Sweet! Perfect! What the hell is the matter with you? A woman is dead in that house. Her body has been decomposing for days. She was all alone. She was sad. You call that 'sweet' and 'perfect'? Don't talk like that." She wrung her hands, looking at the crowd outside. "It's a good thing Mr. Scarfone knows the chief of police. He'll be able to come up with a reason for you touching Mrs. Muldoon's body. Maybe he can say that you were in a state of shock." She turned to look at me in the shadowed car. "What you did was very odd. What in God's name were you thinking, Molly?"

"I wasn't thinking anything *in God's name.*"

She sighed and turned away.

I couldn't understand the big deal everyone was making. We all die. Mrs. Muldoon had chosen her time. I thought she was brave to end her life as she wanted. I didn't think Mrs. Muldoon was sad. That day at the beach was one of the happiest I had ever seen her. I did think it was a bit silly to believe that she would be "going home" to her husband Jim, when she was, in fact, going home to the earth, to her "conqueror worm," a worm that had already begun to feast on her body.

Did she say a prayer for home when she stood in the waves that day and looked towards the horizon? Did she believe that home was somewhere in the sky beyond the sun and clouds?

The image of her body flashed in my mind, and I remembered a poem by Edgar Allan Poe that I had to recite for my English class:

But see, amid the mimic rout,
A crawling shape intrude!
A blood-red thing that writhes from out
The scenic solitude!
It writhes! — it writhes! — with mortal pangs
The mimes become its food,
And the angels sob at vermin fangs
In human gore imbued!

Out — out are the lights — out all!
And, over each dying form,
The curtain, a funeral pall,
Comes down with the rush of a storm,
And the seraphs, all haggard and wan,
Uprising, unveiling, affirm
That the play is the tragedy "Man,"
Its hero the Conqueror Worm.

I thought of the evening Mrs. Muldoon and I talked about the snowflakes falling outside her kitchen window, how no two flakes were exactly alike. On August 15, 1980, Mrs. Muldoon had managed to create something "alike," symmetrical, and balanced through the timing of her death, and that was a kind of beauty, however fleeting. She had created her own assumption and I thought, ironically, *consumption*.

All of this went through my mind as Nonna stared out the window, creating circles of condensation on the glass after sliding away from me on the backseat. The flashing blue light in the heavy air outside was a reminder to all of us that one day we, too, would die. I thought of Aunt Bianca's sullenness, my mother's anxiety, my father's anger and frustration, Nonna's strength and confidence, Mr. Scarfone's mystery, my own indifference. How insignificant all these attributes seemed when faced with the ugliness of death.

In my mind, I heard Mrs. Muldoon singing "Moon River." "We're after the rainbow's end" the song says. But there was no rainbow's end for her. Her end was five days of rot and decay in a hot humid room.

Nonna, as if sensing my thoughts, moved closer, wrapped her arm around me, and rested the side of her warm face on my shoulder.

"Everything will be alright, Molly," she said.

I would like to say that I was comforted, but I wasn't. At that moment, life seemed futile, and prayers for home, wherever we believed we were going, would never be answered. The moon was too high, the river was too wide, and our hearts would be broken after all.

Drenched to the Bone

It has been two years since my ex-wife, Kate, announced that she was unhappy and wanted to end our marriage. I had confronted her about emails from her female lover, Deb, whom she met in yoga class.

Kate said that our relationship lacked passion and if I were honest with myself, I would recognize this truth. In order for both of us to grow, she explained, we needed "clarity in our communication process." Meeting Deb was the beginning of a new phase in her life. A process of individuation, she called it, a term Dr. Kelleher, her Jungian psychologist had used.

"Crisis is good, Jack," she said one morning while we were both getting ready for work. "Both of us have the opportunity for real growth here. I'm sorry that you had to find out this way, but why the hell were you snooping around in my email account?" She looked at me in the mirror as she applied her makeup. Her blue eyes, the first thing that I had noticed about her when we sat across from each other in high school math class, seemed cold and hard.

"The computer geek fixing the hard drive found them. I wasn't looking for anything. I had no reason to be suspicious. I wouldn't invade your personal space." I sat on the edge of the tub, feeling a pit in my stomach, wanting to lash out at her.

She laughed. "Jack, that's just it. You don't even know who I am, what I want. You don't ask me anything. You don't listen. All you ever do is sit in that goddamn chair and read."

"So I read! Jesus, Kate. I'm not a womanizer. I don't drink. I'm home every night with you and the girls. What the fuck did I do wrong?" I could feel my cheeks flush, and my hands were trembling.

She turned and faced me, her hands behind her back, bracing the edge of the sink. "Look, I care about you very much and I don't want to hurt you. But this whole thing isn't working."

"You mean our marriage?"

"Yes. Our marriage."

"You want to end it? Just like that?"

"Jack, I don't want to wake up someday and feel I've wasted my life."

I couldn't believe how cavalier she seemed. "You're saying our marriage has been a waste?" How could this be happening?

"It's nobody's fault. You'll be happier, too. You'll see."

"You can't know that I'll be happier."

"You're right. I can't know." She was suddenly crying. "Because I don't know who you are anymore. You don't talk to me. This is not how I wanted it to be."

"Kate, is it really that bad? I thought it was pretty good."

"Not *bad*. I just need something different, something more. I'm not happy with things the way they are. I'm sorry, Jack, but life is too short for us to be unhappy."

"*I'm* not unhappy."

"But I am." Her voice was tight, and the red spot that appeared on her forehead whenever she was upset was obvious. "You never want to do anything," she said, "I've tried. Really, I've tried." She turned back to the mirror, rifling quickly through her makeup bag. A lipstick rolled into the sink. "If you want to spend your life holed up in this house, you can. Not me." She wasn't looking at me, staring directly into her own face, a face that I had loved for over twenty years. My auburn-haired beauty, I would call her, lightly tracing the line of small freckles over her cheeks and the bridge of her nose with my fingertips, as she laughed and said I was tickling her. I couldn't remember the last time I had done that.

I wanted to say so much. Remind her of everything we had been through, that we had two teenage daughters to consider. But I couldn't speak. Shock, I guess. I tried to convince myself that she was just in a foul mood that day. Maybe she was going through a rough patch in therapy. This, too, would pass, I hoped. Christ! I didn't even give a damn about her lesbian lover. Let her have a fling if it would make her feel better.

But things didn't improve. Eventually I moved out. The divorce became a reality. Our girls, Danielle and Colleen, of course were upset, running through the gamut of emotions, but they, too, came to terms with the change. Danielle would be moving away to college the next fall, and Colleen, a ninth-grader and never very studious, immersed herself in the social aspects of high school.

I have never been one for confrontations or conflict. I gave Kate everything that she wanted in the divorce. Mostly, I just wanted the whole thing over with. I heard that they needed teachers in Florida, and I attended a job fair, where I was offered five jobs in one hour. In August of this past year I began teaching at a school in Fort Lauderdale. I thought a complete change would help me start over, or as Kate would say, "move forward in my spiritual journey."

One day, Deidre Schleppi, a fellow English teacher, and I are walking down the hallway. Someone has smashed the glass front of a vending machine. Bags of Lays potato chips, Doritos, Starbursts, Cheetos, Skittles, and other assorted healthy foods that we provide for our students--lie on the floor in a jumbled mess. Students, laughing and screaming, crouch, dive, slide, and shove each other to get the goods.

"Hey!" I shout. "Get away from there."

When they see Deidre and me, they begin to bolt.

"Fuck you!" a girl in a red dress screams.

By the time we reach the machine, the looters have dispersed. To our amazement, everything is gone except for a ripped bag of skittles, the contents of which are spread across the floor.

"This school is out of control," Deidre says, looking around. "Where the hell is security?"

Ms. Lane comes out of her classroom. "I called the office, guys," she says. "I was eating my lunch in the back of my room when I heard this loud crash. I was scared to death. I didn't dare step outside." She is a beautiful 20-something brunette from El Paso, Texas. Fresh-faced and athletic, she could pass for one of the kids.

In a few moments, Ms. Jackson, our principal, and two maintenance people show up. Cecelia is a demure Latin woman with a broom always in hand, and Carver, a tall, serious man with pale blue eyes and a red stache that he obsessively fingers.

"Did any of you see who did this?" Ms. Jackson's impeccably clean and shiny blond hair glitters like a helmet under the fluorescent light. She's wearing a stylish black business suit and pumps-- probably Gucci, Prada, or some other expensive designer.

"Not exactly. Ms. Schleppi and I were just returning from the cafeteria when we saw a crowd of kids making off with the food. It was a free for all. Reminded me of Filene's Basement at Christmas." I laugh.

All business, Ms. Jackson finds no humor in the situation. She squats down to pick up a big piece of glass. To Cecelia and Carver she says, "If a student cuts himself, we could have ourselves a terrible lawsuit." She waves the glass in the air. Cecelia ducks slightly, as though she thinks Ms. Jackson might scratch her with it. "I want this thing moved and the whole area swept thoroughly.

"You English teachers," she says to the rest of us, "need to have more of a presence in the hallway. I'd appreciate it if you check the hallway periodically and keep an eye on which students use the vending machine. We all should be vigilant."

I look around the dimly lit hall with its pea-green floors and beat-down blue lockers and think, Shit. Another pain-in-the-ass thing to do. When do we get to teach?

"Will that be a problem?"

"Yeah, I have a problem," Deidre says. "Where's security? Why aren't they up here during lunch. It's not the teachers' responsibility to patrol the campus." Her face is red.

"Some of the students are pretty disruptive," I say. "Something's gotta be done." I can feel my own anger rising.

"Look. I understand where you guys are coming from. But security can't do it alone. I need the cooperation of my teachers."

Ms. Lane says, "Isn't anybody watching the cameras?" She points to the camera at the end of the hall.

"Well, sure. They're supposed to be. On my way up here, I checked with Ms. Vickman. Evidently, she screwed up. She didn't have the damn camera on, or it's broken, or God knows what's wrong with the system. I promise you I'll check into it. By the end of the week, I'll have this fixed," she says, patting the side of the vending machine, "and I'll be watching the cameras myself."

The period bell rings and students begin to enter the corridor. Ms. Jackson pushes her way through a group of flashy Latin girls who mutter under their breath "bitch" and "fat ass," but Jackson either doesn't hear, or chooses to ignore them.

The next day I teach "Civil Disobedience" to my English Three class.

As always, it takes a while to get the students settled. When I tell them to put their cell phones, iPods, and any other electronic devices away, I always feel like the classroom is about to take off. I'm the flight attendant and they are my passengers.

"Put all book bags underneath your desks and open your textbooks to page 370."

I start to read Thoreau's essay aloud. The kids are talking over me. A few haven't opened their books yet. Eventually though, the class settles down, becomes less frenetic, and some are listening. Mostly, they don't understand the turgid prose, so I have to stop every few sentences and paraphrase. When I get to the sentence, "The only obligation which I have a right to assume is to do at any time what I think right," Leo Turpin, one of the chronic nappers, raises his hand. The other kids think he is cool and call him "Turp."

"So this guy is saying that we don't have to do what other people tell us?" He leans back in his chair, smirking.

"In a way, Leo. Thoreau is talking about an individual's conscience as being the most important aspect of who we are. You remember Emerson? 'Nothing is at last sacred but the integrity of your own mind' and his other quote, 'What have I to do with the sacredness of traditions, if I live wholly from within?' " He looks clueless, as do most of the others.

Brandi, a heavyset black girl who is always writing about her diabetes, raises her hand. "Isn't he the guy that invented electricity?"

"You're talking about Edison. He invented the light bulb. Good point though." I don't think it's a good point, but sometimes you lie because at least students are listening and some semblance of a discussion has begun.

Darren from the back shouts, "What page?"

Sandy, a quiet Pakistani girl next to him, points to the paragraph in his book. Sandy types are blessings.

Beneatha by the back window says, "I gotta use the bathroom."

"Not now," I say firmly.

"Mr. . . . " She looks around, confused. I hear her say to Reggie under her breath, "What's his name?" I have been her teacher for four months.

"Mr. McCarthy, if you don't let me go, my pussy's gonna burst." This is followed by laughter from the others.

"You better go," I say. 'And don't be such a smartass with that mouth of yours."

Amelia and Brandi are whispering. Then Amelia raises her

hand.

"I like this guy," she says. At first I think she is going to tell us about another boyfriend who broke her heart, but I am jubilant to realize she is talking about Thoreau. "It's cool what he says about government and how we don't need one."

Brandi adds, "Yeah, why should we have to follow laws if we don't agree with them? We should only have to listen to our own conscious. No one has a right to tell us how to think or what we should do."

"It's *conscience,* you moron," Mary Grace, a pimple-faced obese white girl from Georgia shouts from the back of the room. She is always reading. Lately, she is consumed with the Bible. She told me she was going to finish it by the end of the school year. "And Mr. McCarthy, I don't think living by yourself in the woods for two years like Thoreau did is healthy. I think he was a narcissist."

"What's a narcissist?" Brandi asks.

"It's a person that is really into himself. Very self-centered."

Mary Grace snickers and opens Flannery O'Connor's *Wise Blood.* I don't care that she rarely pays attention to what we are reading in class. She is far ahead of the other students.

"Amelia and Brandi both make good points," I add. "Thoreau thinks our *conscience* is very important. An individual, according to him, should have the freedom to disobey a law that his conscience tells him is unjust. He's saying that it is really important for us to speak up if we have decided that something isn't right. What would happen, though, if we all decided to ignore the laws that we disagreed with? And what would happen if we didn't have any laws at all? If we didn't pay attention to what other people needed and just lived for ourselves?"

Brandi says, "Everyone should just do what they want. We shouldn't have to follow rules if we think they're dumb. It's messed up."

"This school is like a prison," Amelia says, and the other members of the class are suddenly very interested.

Someone says, "Yeah. Fuck this place."

"Hey! Watch your language," I say.

"Then bits of black dust begin to spew out of the air conditioning vent next to the American flag.

"What's that?" Trisha, a student prone to hysteria, screams.

"Mr.! There's black shit all over my desk," Mike says.

"Lily you got some in your hair!" Vega jumps up and points.

Lily pushes her hands through her hair and screams. "Oh my God!"

The fire alarm goes off and I manage to guide my class along the corridor and down the east stairwell to the designated area of lawn behind the school. After accounting for all my students who meet me under a fichus tree, I walk over to Deidre and Ms. Lane, who are leaning against a chain-link fence by a section of dead grass.

"Stupid bastards," Deidre says. "They are working on the roof and they forget to turn off the ventilation system. All of us breathing in that tar. That stuff is so carcinogenic."

"Really?" Lane gasps. "Cancer runs in my family. Like I need any more risk factors." She puts her hand over her mouth, and looks visibly distressed.

"Look at her," Deidre says, pointing to Jackson who is yelling up at two roofers descending a ladder by the auditorium. "I'm sure she's giving them hell. Probably worried about another lawsuit. Forget about the health of the faculty and students." She shakes her head.

"She's not so bad," Lane says. "It's not her fault that they fucked up. Can't blame her for everything. She's got a lot on her plate." Lane looks smug, like she knows something we don't.

"What do you mean?" I ask.

"I was talking to her secretary, Elsa. She said Jackson has a mother at home with dementia and a brother who doesn't do anything but hang out all day. He's unemployed. Never even finished high school. She said Jackson's been getting a lot of calls from neighbors who find her mother wandering around the neighborhood. Her brother is usually stoned in his room. A total loser."

Brandi and Amelia come running over to us.

"Is the school on fire?" Brandi asks excitedly.

"No, but we'll probably all get cancer," Deidre mumbles, then laughs.

I explain to the students about the tar and tell them not to worry. "I'm sure they'll clean it all up."

Carver and Cecelia have joined Jackson and the roofers. Jackson is giving the two of them some directives. They nod their heads, ask a couple questions, and then head into the building. Jackson takes her radio from her waist and says something. A few minutes later, Ms. Vickman and two other security guards make the rounds among the crowd of faculty and students. We are told that we'll be allowed to enter the building in about twenty minutes, once the maintenance crew has had a chance to clean up. The students are disappointed that the school didn't go up in a blaze.

"They don't care about us," Amelia says. "We could get cancer and die."

I explain to the kids that their chances of getting cancer from this one incident are slim.

"Uh-uh," Brandi says. "This ain't right. It's like that guy Walden said."

"You mean Thoreau," I say.

"Yeah him. This is a type of injustice. We should break a law or something." She's smiling and wide-eyed.

"Yeah. We should stage some kinda civil obedience," Amelia adds. "Make a big statement."

"*Disobedience*. You dumbass," Brandi says.

I decide to teach a less political text the next day so I choose what I think is a benign piece by Langston Hughes called "Salvation," a bittersweet essay in which Hughes recounts his childhood attendance at a church revival and the "special meeting for children 'to bring the young lambs to the fold' " at the end of the service. Most of my students come from religious backgrounds so I think they will be able to relate. In the essay, Hughes relays his anxiety and frustration as he "kept waiting to see Jesus," how he believed that Jesus would literally come into the church and walk down the aisle. That night he cried over his deception, when after waiting an interminable amount of time during which his "aunt came and knelt at [his] knees and cried, while prayers and songs swirled all around [him] in the little church," he finally approached the altar, pretending to "see" Jesus come, joining the fold of "little lambs" (his tired peers) who had already been "saved."

The reading of this essay creates an animated discussion about beliefs. Kayla, one of my favorites, announces, "I have a question about the Bible. Are we supposed to believe that Jonah was swallowed by a whale and lived inside that thing for three days? Cause I think that's crazy! I don't believe that junk is true, Mr. McCarthy. Is it true?" And she looks at me with an adamant cause-I-just-really-gotta-know expression on her face, as though I will end her confusion right then and there.

I answer, as teachers are supposed to respond, respectful of the students, many of whom come from Biblical literalist religious traditions, that people read the Bible in different ways: some believe that it is the literal word of God, and others believe that the stories are meant to be understood symbolically. In America, I add, we believe in tolerance, and respect the diversity of religious beliefs.

Vega, who is seated at the back of the room, bursts into laughter at something she is remembering. She jumps up and down in her seat, and exclaims, "Jesus came into my church this weekend."

She runs to the front of the room, sits down, and begins her story, fluttering her hand in front of her mouth, excited in her recollection, laughing, her white teeth shining. "There's this homeless guy. He thinks he's Jesus."

The class explodes with laughter. Brandi, Amelia, and others said, "I know him!" They exchange stories of this man, discussing how he's made the rounds in their churches.

Vega continues, "He just walked in, said he was Jesus, and started rollin' on the floor. We were all singin' and the pastor, he just ignored him. I wanted to laugh, but I knew my mother would kill me." I, like Vega's classmates, find the story amusing, so I prod her. I want the details, trying to picture the reactions of the congregation more completely.

"No one did anything? They just ignored him?" I ask.

"Yeah." She laughs. "We didn't want to disrespect him. We just carried on!"

The other students share their anecdotes, and then I bring the class back to order, back to our discussion of Hughes's "Salvation." Students draw comparisons between their individual religious experiences and those of Langston Hughes.

Turpin wakes from his nap and says, "I don't believe Jesus even existed. And how can someone pay for our sins by getting nailed to a cross? That shit don't make sense." He grins, looking around the classroom for approval. "Turp" is the unspoken leader among his peers. Students are afraid to disagree with him.

Mike says, "Yeah. I don't believe any of that stuff either. It's a bunch of propaganda to keep the masses under control. I read that somewhere. The oxycodone of the masses." He smiles and nods his head.

"You mean *opium* of the people. What Karl Marx, a famous philosopher, actually said was 'Religion is the sigh of the oppressed creature, the heart of a heartless world and the soul of soulless conditions. It is the opium of the people.' "

"You're so smart, Mr. McCarthy. How do you remember all those quotes?" Amelia says.

"I read a lot, and all of you should, too. Reading helps make you a free thinker."

Mary Grace says, "You can read all you want but it won't make you a better person. You need to act in the world, not retire from it like Thoreau. Helping others is what God wants us to do."

Sandy, who barely speaks in class, pipes up, "I agree with Mary Grace." She glances at Leo and Mike. "And free thinking should not allow people to make fun of others' beliefs." Then she slouches on her desk, looking sheepish.

"I have a right to say whatever I want, Sandy," Turp says. "Like that guy Edison said."

Mary Grace puts down O'Connor's novel, her face bright red. She takes off her glasses; her eyes twitch, and her forehead is sweating. "It's *Emerson.* And you're all as dumb as rocks, especially you *Turd!*"

Beneatha, who sits in the desk in front of her, quickly asks to go to the bathroom. When she passes my desk, she whispers, "That white girl's crazy" and hurries out of the room.

"Fuck you, you fat ugly bitch!" Turp says and laughs. Mike laughs, too. The girls in the room look at Mary Grace with both pity and fear.

Mary Grace snaps her teeth and turns down her lip. She throws her psychology textbook at Turpin and almost hits him in the head. Luckily, he dodges and the book hits the wall. "You are all a bunch of pigs, especially you, Turd. And you're no better than Turd, Mr. McCarthy. I know you think that because you're a teacher you know everything, but you don't! I read, but I pray, too. And I try to help other people by going to church and reaching out to others."

Turpin laughs. "Admit it. You go to church because you have no friends. Get a life." He looks at his peers with a big grin.

Mary Grace charges Turpin and some of the students run for the door. The girls scream. Mary Grace begins choking Turpin; his face blanches. I press the emergency alarm and dial security at the same time. Mike pulls the two apart, managing to free Turpin from Mary Grace, who kneels on the floor and places her hands together in prayer: "Do not give dogs what is holy, and do not throw your pearls before pigs, lest they trample them underfoot and turn to attack you.'

" Then she stands on her chair, looking up at the ugly water-stained ceiling tiles, hands raised, a crazed look on her face. "We are all sinners and the wages of sin is death, but the free gift of God is eternal life in Christ Jesus our Lord."

The security guy, Mr. Pierre, enters, a tall black guy with dreadlocks. He glimpses Mary Grace, then looks at me and raises his eyebrows. I nod. Beneatha returns from the bathroom, standing behind him, as if for protection. "I told you that girl was crazy, Mr. She thinks that she's Joan of *Narc*. I'm getting out of here. Types like her might have a gun. It's always the Caucasian kids who go nuts and shoot everyone up." The remaining students follow her, hurrying out of the room.

"Don't worry, Mr. McCarthy. I'll get them to return," Mr. Pierre says. Mary Grace is surprisingly quiet and well behaved now, a strange smile on her face.

"Come with me, young lady," Mr. Pierre says.

She puts her glasses on and begins to follow him out the door.

"Could you take Leo Turpin to the office and make sure he's okay? He looked fine, but Mary Grace really went after him."

"Sure. I got your back." He has a kind smile.

I sit at my desk, trying to absorb what has just happened. The experience unnerved me. And it wasn't so much the chaos. Mary Grace, as deranged as she had acted, uttered a truth about me. I did think I knew a lot. I did keep to myself. In the stillness of the classroom, I sit at my desk, looking out at the swaying palm trees and clouded sky. Some droplets began to fall on the vegetation.

Soon the students return, ushered in by Mr. Pierre. I thank him and tell the class to spend the rest of the period reading quietly. I fill out the necessary paperwork to document what has happened, but am preoccupied by what Mary Grace said, reflecting on my arrogance and self-centeredness.

That afternoon, I stay late to put grades into the computer, which is a rarity for me. I'm usually one of the first to leave. When I exit the building, the parking lot is nearly empty. In the far corner, behind the cafeteria dumpster, I spot Jackson, who waves for me to come over. She's staring at the side of her silver Audi as I approach.

"Look at this."

Someone has keyed her car from front to back on the driver's side.

"Well that sucks," I say, rubbing my hand over a portion of the scratch. Then I see where the vandal etched 'bitch.'

"At least they spelled it right." Jackson laughs.

"You can check these cameras, can't you?" I point to them and wonder if the car scratching is Brandi and Amelia's doing, a bit of civil disobedience. I'm pissed at the monsters I might have created.

"Nope. The entire surveillance system is down. I have a service person coming tomorrow. It seems everything's falling apart. Everything's broken. Can't even park in my designated spot because of the burst pipe in front of the school. God knows when they'll be through with that project. I thought my car would be safe over here, off the beaten track."

"Nothing's safe anymore," I say.

"You can say that again." She leans against the hood of the car and takes a cigarette out of her purse. "You want one?"

"Nah. I don't smoke."

"One of my vices. Helps me with the stress." She lights up, then exhales slowly. "I know the kids hate me. Most of the faculty, too. But I'm just trying to do my job. Keep things running smoothly, maybe make a few improvements. Get us the money we need. You understand that, don't you?"

"Of course."

Her cellphone rings and she takes it out of her back pocket, then steps away while holding up her index finger. She speaks softly into the phone. Her expression is strained and serious.

When she's finished, she says, "My mother. She keeps asking for me. That was the aide who looks in on her a couple times a week. Alzheimer's is a horrible disease. Do you have anyone in your family with it?"

"No. Well at least not yet."

"Good." She tamps her cigarette out against the side of the dumpster, then flicks it inside. "I wouldn't wish that disease on anyone. Watching someone lose their mind is awful, Jack." I'm surprised by her use of my first name.

"It must be difficult for you."

"My mother isn't who she used to be. She was a strong woman, very independent. I wish I had asked her more questions when she was well. I wish I had taken the time to talk to her. *Really* talk to her. We spend too much time in our own heads. There is so much I wish I knew about her life, but it's too late. If only I had asked." She is staring at something in the distance. Then she nods her head, not to me, but to something she is thinking. "I miss her." She sighs and looks into my face. Her eyes are rheumy. "But we all have our problems. Your day wasn't so great either. I suspended Mary Grace for two weeks and had Elsa set up an appointment with the school psychologist."

"I'm glad. That poor girl needs help. Thank you."

"Thank *you* for coming over. I needed to vent."

"We can all use a little of that."

"I'm outta here," she says, opening her car door. "You should go home, too. Before you get drenched." She looks up. "That sky looks ominous." A flash of lightening zigzags in the sky beyond her.

On the way home, I think about the chaos and brokenness that surrounds me—the tumult in my classroom, the ridiculous vending machine, the cameras that do not work, Jackson's mother wandering and getting lost, my failed marriage, even my aging body. The thought of all these things depresses me.

It begins to rain hard now, as is often the case during South Florida afternoons. People dodge puddles as they hurry across the street, some with umbrellas, others holding bags over their heads. When I pass the church on the corner of 26th Street and 15th avenue, the rain is pelting, obscuring the road in front of me. I drive into the parking lot to wait it out and read the large quote on the entry sign. The irony in the words of St. Francis strikes me: "We have been called to heal wounds, to unite what has fallen apart, and to bring home those who have lost their way."

But could my wounds, or those of anyone else, ever be really healed? And isn't it a law of physics that objects in our world eventually fall apart: entropy, the gradual decline into disorder leading ultimately to the death of our universe. Galaxies are floating further and further away, drifting into the infinity of space. That is alienation, not unity. On this October day, so much of life seems "fallen apart," spiraling into an inevitable state of decline.

What exactly is *the way*? Who will tell us? Had Mary Grace been trying to tell *me*? Kate? Maybe I *was* too self-absorbed during our marriage. *"You don't ask me anything. You don't listen. . . . I don't know who you are anymore. You don't talk to me,"* she had said. My eyes begin to burn. I realize that even *I* am not sure who I am. Midway through my life, I am lost.

These are my thoughts as I sit in the steeple-shadowed parking lot. I put the wipers on high and rub the inside of the fogged-up windshield. Lightening crackles across the dark horizon. I wait.

Soon the time between the thundering lengthens, and the intense rain begins to diminish. I hope that before long I will be able to see the way home. When the rain starts to abate, I put the wipers on low and turn the radio to a station that plays classics from the sixties. I increase the volume in an attempt to block out my uncomfortable thoughts. As I ease out of the parking lot, I read the other side of the sign: "Will you follow the road to experience God's salvation and have eternal life? Join us Sundays 9 am and 11 am."

I turn onto 15th Street, where pools of water continue to grow from rain that is falling, but more softly now. The light is red at the next intersection. I dial Kate on my cellphone.

"Hi Jack," she says.

"Kate, I'm sorry. I should have paid more attention to you."

The light changes to green. Bob Dylan sings,

Come gather 'round people
Wherever you roam
And admit that the waters
Around you have grown
And accept it that soon
You'll be drenched to the bone
If your time to you is worth savin'
Then you better start swimmin' or you'll sink like a stone
For the times they are a-changin'

"I'm also responsible for the problems we had. Don't blame it all on yourself. I'm sorry, Jack. . . .Hey, I like that song. It reminds me of when we were young."

"Tell me about you, Kate."

48967425R00071

Made in the USA
Lexington, KY
19 January 2016